HOUSE OF SPIES

By the same author

Danger at the Doghouse
River of Secrets
Second Sight
The Silent Pool

For more information about Griselda Gifford's books see: www.griselda.co.uk

HOUSE OF SPIES

Griselda Gifford

Andersen Press · London

To Jim and the family

With many thanks to my editor, Audrey Adams,
and my agent, Pat White.

The author thanks Mr Terry Charman of the Imperial War
Museum for his help.

First published in 2005 by
Andersen Press Limited,
20 Vauxhall Bridge Road, London SWIV 2SA
www.andersenpress.co.uk

British Library Cataloguing in Publication Data available

ISBN 1 84270 459 1

Typeset by FiSH Books, Enfield, Middlesex
Printed and bound in Great Britain by Bookmarque Ltd.,
Croydon, Surrey

Chapter 1

I could hear the thud, thud of bombs falling but I couldn't move. My legs were pinned to the bed. I had to get down to the cellar. I had to be safe from the bombs...

Someone was shaking me. 'Wake up!' Mum said and the weight on my feet shifted as Thomasina, our cat, leaped off and out of the window. I wasn't in our flat by the sea but here in the cottage where we were supposed to be safe from the Germans invading, even though there wasn't an air-raid shelter. How I hated this horrible war, changing everything.

A voice from the hall was shouting at us to hurry.

'Pip – get dressed!' Mum said, pulling a jumper over my head as if I were a little kid. 'It's an unexploded bomb.' She was wearing a coat over her nightie. 'Get your shoes and your gas mask on the way out,' she said.

I grabbed the mouse cage and heard a skittering of tiny paws as Josephine and Joshua tried to keep their balance inside.

'Come on!' Mum shouted – she hardly ever shouted so I knew we were in danger.

Still blurry from sleep I found I was in the hall.

'Hurry,' said a man I couldn't see properly because the light of his torch pointed down at my feet. 'Shoes,'

1

he said. I thrust my feet into my wellies because I didn't want to do up shoelaces. Then I stopped. 'But we've got to find Thomasina first.'

The man seized my arm and marched Mum and me out of Rose Cottage and into the road. The policeman's thin beam of torch swung a moment so I could see a black hole across the lane, just in front of Nurse Robin's cottage. 'It's a good thing the bomb didn't go off,' he said.

'Is Nurse Robinson all right?' I asked, my heart thumping. Nurse Robin always seemed so busy and alive, cycling off every day to visit her patients. She had a funny way of holding her head on one side when you met her and looking carefully at you with her small black eyes. Her black-stockinged legs were bird-thin. Robin fitted her just right, I thought.

'Just shaken up,' he said. 'She's gone ahead with the Warden.'

'But the bomb could go off any time and Thomasina won't know about evacuating,' I said, trying not to cry.

'She'll be fine,' Mum said calmly. 'The soldiers will come tomorrow to take the bomb away. Don't worry, Pipkin. She'll be all right.'

We were hurried down the lane, following Miss Robinson, to Hogsty End High Street where the police-man knocked on the door of the Sow and Pigs, the village pub. The landlord, Mr Jarvis, took us all in.

His wife smothered Nurse Robin in a blanket and almost pushed her into a chair in the beer-smelling bar. The nurse peeped out of the blanket, a pink hairnet over her curlers. She looked even more like a baby bird when

2

she opened her toothless mouth. 'My false teeth!' she moaned. 'That horrible bomb falling blew away the glass they were in and I've lost them.' Then she saw the mouse cage. Josephine Pie, whiskers quivering, was holding the bars in her small pink paws and staring at Nurse Robin, who screeched, 'Don't bring those creatures near me!'

'Josephine and Joshua won't hurt you,' I said. 'They're very intelligent and never bite. I'm teaching them to walk along a string tightrope.'

Nurse Robin gave a smothered cry and Mrs Jarvis soothed her with a cup of tea. 'I'll make up the beds for you,' she said.

'Won't they take the bomb away tonight?' I asked, half-knowing it was a silly question.

'Don't fuss, darling,' Mum said, calmly drinking her tea. The hairnet she wore at night had slipped to one side and her frilly nightie showed under her coat but she behaved as if we'd been asked out to a polite tea party.

She never seemed to be scared. I remembered that time two months ago when we were walking on the cliffs, the sea glittering blue below. There was the throb of a plane above and Mum pulled me down to the ground. I looked up and saw the German markings – a black cross under the plane's wings – as it swooped low. Then it flew off.

'Thank goodness I knitted us green jumpers,' Mum said as we hurried back home. 'Almost matched the grass.'

When the bombs came, mostly in the daytime, we

went down to the basement of the block of flats and I got into trouble for letting the mice out. The other people sheltering with us screamed so loudly it almost drowned the thud of the bombs and the rattle of the guns. Why are people scared of mice? I love the feeling of their small feet as they run down my arm and the way they stop and wash their faces with tiny pink paws.

When Dad got a day's leave from the RAF and drove us away from the coast, I wasn't too sorry because the seaside was disappointing. Rolls of barbed wire and concrete 'pill boxes' stopped us going on the beach and that was the whole point of the seaside. Dad said he'd drive far away, to where things were safer but I was so car-sick that he had to stop at Hogsty End, a village only an hour from London. We'd been living in London until a year ago when the war began.

Poor Thomasina had moved from London to the seaside and now to the country. She was like me, moved about like a parcel because of the war but at least she didn't have to go to *another* new school in September.

I didn't sleep much that night because I was so worried about Thomasina and I woke up hearing the first birds twittering and the unfamiliar sound of cocks crowing. When I drew the blackout curtains I saw the pearl-grey of early morning.

I had to see if they'd moved the bomb. Mum was fast asleep and didn't stir while I dressed – well, put my jumper over my pyjamas and my feet into the wellies. I did wish my pyjamas hadn't got little sprigs of pink flowers all over them but I wasn't likely to see anyone.

4

My rubber soles muffled the sound as I crept past the other bedrooms, hearing snores.

I went through the smelly bar. They'd left the key in the lock so I opened the front door and ran up the street. There was a clatter of bottles and clopping of hooves as the milkman's cart drove past but nobody else was about.

As I turned the corner to our lane, an Army lorry rumbled past so close I had to squash into the hedge. It stopped ahead of me and soldiers leaped out.

I saw there was barbed wire across the top of the lane and a notice: DANGER – UNEXPLODED BOMB.

Thomasina was a crouching splodge on the sagging tiles of our cottage. She stood up, waving her tail in distress, and I could see her mouth opening as she wailed but I was too far off to hear her.

'Please can I fetch my cat?' I said to one of the soldiers standing by the wire.

He actually laughed at me. 'You off your head, girl? If that bomb explodes you'll be dead meat.'

I hated him. 'It'll be all your fault if our cat starves to death or gets blown up.'

'Go home to your mum, little girl – and get dressed proper!' The soldiers were all laughing at me. 'Little girl' – and I'm a teenager! I wish I could say I walked away with dignity but I didn't. I made a rude sign and ran back to the High Street, holding up my pyjamas as the elastic was loose.

As I came to the corner, a grey pony coming up the hill swerved and its rider shouted at me. 'Look where you're going!'

He was a boy of about my age, his dirty bare feet dangling below the pony's sides. 'Mind out yourself!' I yelled.

'Fancy wearing pyjamas in the daytime!' he jeered.

At that moment a motorbike roared up the hill towards the soldiers. The pony leaped sideways and the boy hurtled into the ditch.

When the pony turned and came trotting past me, ears back, I snatched at a loop of rein and pulled so hard that the leather hurt my hand. I hung on, thinking of the convoys of Army lorries we'd seen coming through the village since we came. The pony wouldn't stand a chance if it got out on the main road.

I'd read pony stories and longed to ride. There were even shameful memories of sitting on a swinging branch to which I'd tied reins and pretended I was galloping. But of course that was when I was much younger.

'Steady, boy,' I said, like they did in books.

Amazingly, the pony stood still and as I stroked his sweating neck he nudged at me, his sharp whiskers prickling my face.

The boy was climbing out of the ditch, pulling burrs off his shorts. His face was muddy and scratched. 'Thanks,' he said. 'You can let go now,' and took the reins. He paused, leaning against the pony, wiping the back of his hand over his face and making it worse. 'So what are you doing in those daft pyjamas?' he asked again.

'There's an unexploded bomb by our cottage up the lane.' I pointed.

'I heard. I came to have a look. Also, we've lost

Auntie, our goat. I thought she might have wandered up that way through the woods.'

'You aren't allowed there. The beastly soldiers won't let me past and I must rescue poor Thomasina.'

He looked at me curiously, his hair standing on end where he'd pulled out the brambles. 'Who's Thomasina?'

'Our cat.'

'Cats fend for themselves. Ours catch mice, rats and all. We just give them a bowl of milk.'

'Thomasina's only been here a few weeks and she's a town cat. Besides, she might get blown up. And she won't know we're at the Sow and Pigs.'

He actually laughed at me. 'She won't starve for a couple of days.'

I was annoyed. 'We came from the coast and she might try to find her way back.'

He slung himself onto the pony's back. 'Tell you what. Go up at night when nobody's looking. Bet we could find a way through.'

'You want to come?'

'Yeah. Might find the goat. And it would be fun. See you here, as soon as it's dark. I'll bring a torch. What's your name? Mine's Harry.'

'Pippa – but Mum won't let me . . . ' I began but he dug his heels into the pony's sides and trotted off.

Chapter 2

'Don't worry, Pip,' Mum said for the hundredth time that day. 'Thomasina will be all right. She'll catch mice.'

I had the mouse cage outside with us in the pub garden. It was another hot day and we sat in the shade of an apple tree.

I looked at the mice, glad they couldn't understand Mum. *They* wouldn't miss Thomasina, who usually spent some of her time looking up at the mouse cage, licking her lips. The black and white mouse, Josephine Pie, stopped halfway down the ladder from the mouse bedroom and stared at me, her red eyes gleaming like jewels. Her shy husband, Joshua, had retreated to the safety of their small upstairs bedroom.

'You know Thomasina's old and fat. She'd only catch mice if they were on crutches or something,' I said crossly, scratching my back under the man's shirt Mrs Jarvis had loaned me. It was stiff with starch and most uncomfortable.

'The soldier was quite definite when I talked to him,' Mum said. 'They just wouldn't let me past.'

She'd insisted on going up there alone and leaving me polishing glasses for Mrs Jarvis, who was short-handed now her husband had joined something called the Local Defence Volunteers, who were going to fight the

Germans if we were invaded.

Mum had been asleep when I came back earlier and still didn't know I'd been out. As I was planning to meet Harry in the evening, I thought I'd not tell her – unless they took the bomb away this afternoon.

Mum had wavy black hair and big brown eyes. She was pretty and still fairly young. If she couldn't get past the soldiers, nobody else would. 'They'll make it safe as soon as the bomb disposal experts come,' she said, knitting furiously. As well as our gas masks and a small case she'd brought her precious knitting bag out of the cottage.

She always knitted faster when she was worried. It was another jumper for me: made out of many unpicked old woollies and doomed to be in horrible multi-coloured stripes again. 'Mrs Jarvis says we can stay another night, provided you don't let the mice out again.' Mum looked at me reproachfully. 'I suppose poor Nurse Robinson will be stuck here too. It's a good thing she's gone out to see her patients to take her mind off it.'

'She looked funny in Mrs Jarvis's old dress, didn't she? I saw her on that rusty bike they lent her and the dress was so long she had to tuck it up.'

Mum looked at me reprovingly. 'I think she's very brave going to work after such a shock. Especially without her false teeth.'

I giggled and she couldn't help joining in. 'We're being unkind,' she said. 'She's very kind and helps lots of people.'

I stopped giggling and felt gloomy. 'If the bomb goes off, we'll all be homeless. And it's more difficult for us,

9

with the mice and Thomasina. I don't see why nobody likes mice. They need exercise and it's not their fault there's a stupid war on.'

Mum stopped knitting. 'Pippa! Don't sulk. And you're quite old enough to understand why we're fighting. The Germans have invaded most of Europe and they want to come here next. You wouldn't want Germans marching through the village, would you? And Hitler in Buckingham Palace?'

I tried to imagine Germans goose-stepping through Hogsty End and Hitler sitting on the Royal throne. He'd probably put the poor King and Queen in the Tower and chop their heads off. And what would happen to the poor Princesses? I shivered. 'No.'

Mum put the knitting away in her silky pink bag. 'Now, put the mice back in your room. Mrs Jarvis has gone to the shop so you won't meet her. It was a pity you let them out just when she came up with tea for us.'

Mrs Jarvis had come in just as Josephine Pie was washing her ears on the dressing table, in front of the mirror – probably admiring herself. There hadn't been any need for Mrs Jarvis to scream or drop the tea. You'd think in the country people would be used to mice.

I felt a fool wearing Joe Jarvis's long grey shorts. Joe was away in the Army now, but once he'd been a fat boy, so the waistband was all bundled round by a leather belt which made me feel hot. Mrs Jarvis hadn't found any shoes to fit me so I still wore my wellies.

Mum and I went up to the barbed wire barricade again and called Thomasina but she wasn't on the roof and she didn't come. I had a nasty thought that she might be inside the house where she'd be trapped if the bomb went off.

A grey-haired soldier was on duty – Mum said he was a Local Defence Volunteer. I was glad as the other soldier might have told Mum I'd been up there. He said the bomb people would probably come the next day. 'You're not to worry, Missus. They're very skilful at defusing bombs,' he said.

Mum sent me to the village shop and Post Office to buy paper so she could write to Dad and she gave me two pennies to buy sweets. 'Make the most of it,' she said. 'They'll be rationed soon.'

The shop was small with an ancient bottle-glass window, now crisscrossed with tape in case of bombs. Inside it was plastered with patriotic notices: CARE-LESS TALK COSTS LIVES; WALLS HAVE EARS; DIG FOR VICTORY; BE LIKE DAD, KEEP MUM.

I don't think the shopkeeper, a plump old lady with white hair screwed up into a bun, had really read the notices because she immediately asked me about the bomb and then about Dad. 'He's a bomber pilot,' I said, wondering if that was CARELESS TALK.

'Ah – now, tell your mother there's a group of us meets at the Vicarage to make curtains for Wellington bombers. We'd be glad of another pair of hands.'

I wondered if the curtains were all flowery to make the aircrew feel cosy and at home. I bought a Sherbet Sucker – a hollow liquorice stick to suck up the fizzy sherbet at the end – and a giant humbug.

11

Mrs Jarvis gave us high tea, which was Spam and potato pie followed by rhubarb and custard. I scooped a bit of Spam into my handkerchief as a lure for Thomasina. We finished with the usual wartime grey bread with almost no marg and rhubarb jam. I couldn't eat much because I was worrying about Thomasina and anyway, I don't eat a lot, that's why I'm fairly thin.

Nurse Robin twittered on, giving us gory details about bandaging an old man's leg and saying how upset all her patients had been to hear about her cottage. I tried not to look at her bare gums, chewing the food.

The washing-up seemed to take ages and Mrs Jarvis was short-handed because her husband was still out with the Defence Volunteers on a practice. 'Although I don't know what that bunch of oldish men and a few flat-footed young ones would do if we were invaded, I'm sure,' she said. 'There aren't even enough guns for them so some have imitation wooden guns. They're nicknamed the "Look, Duck and Vanish" and I reckon that's just about right.'

So Mum helped serve at the bar. I heard her laughing as she pulled the beer-handles and over-filled glasses and I was pleased because she hadn't laughed a great deal lately.

I sat in the kitchen writing my letter to Dad but at the same time wondering how I was going to slip out.

Mum came in and I yawned hard and she said she wanted to listen to the News with Nurse Robin and Mrs Jarvis. That was another boring thing about the war – everyone was always listening to the News. She said I'd better get to bed.

I exercised and fed the mice and then got into bed with

my clothes on. I didn't mean to sleep but I suppose I must have done because there was a bell and a loud voice in the bar and sounds of people banging the door as they went out. Later I heard Mum come upstairs. She put her head round the door and I pretended to be asleep. I gave her time to settle and crept downstairs, carrying a torch.

I unbolted the front door, worrying at the loud noise it made.

The street seemed pitch dark at first because every curtain was tight shut. Then my eyes got used to it. I saw the stars high in the sky and walked towards our turning.

Harry wouldn't be there, I was sure. He was the sort of boy who made wild promises. The barbed wire and the soldier's gun glinted in the moonlight.

Suddenly a hand grabbed my arm and I jumped.

'You're late,' Harry said. 'Follow me.'

I scrambled after him, up the bank and through a scratchy hole in the hedge. Then he ran up the side of a field, doubled over rather unnecessarily as the soldier wasn't likely to look over the hedge.

'Here!' I whispered and we climbed over our fence and we were in the back garden which sloped steeply down to our cottage. From here, looking through a gap in the hedge, I could just see the lane below and Nurse Robin's cottage with the dark hole by her front door.

I called Thomasina quietly. She didn't come so we pushed through the bushes and down to the bit Mum had dug to grow vegetables. So far, there were just a few seedlings and someone else's runner beans.

13

Was that a dark, horned creature walking out of the beansticks? I drew back.

'That's our goat!' Harry said, running forward.

Then I saw the crouched shape of Thomasina on top of the roof of the outside lavatory. I called her and she jumped down, running to me with a little mewing sound. I picked her up quickly and made soothing noises so she didn't run away. I'd decided I'd got to get her back to the Sow and Pigs, whatever Mrs Jarvis might say.

I heard a sound behind us and looked round. A thin thread of torchlight showed the figure of a boy running towards us. 'Come back, goat!' he called.

I clutched Thomasina as the boy ran straight down the twisty cottage path, out of the gate and across the lane.

'He can't go there!' Harry ran, towing a pale shape by a chain and I ran after him, still carrying Thomasina, who scratched me as she struggled to escape.

I ran past Harry. The moon slipped out of clouds and now I saw the boy looking down at the gleaming fins of the bomb. The moonlight shone on his pale hair. I shouted, 'Look out! It might go off!'

He turned but didn't move. I ran and grabbed his arm with my free hand, pulling him away but he twisted out of my grasp, ran straight down the lane to the barbed wire, and disappeared through a gap.

'Catch him!' I heard Harry call and then Thomasina leaped from under my arm and ran in the same direction. I went after her, forgetting the soldier, calling her name.

'Stop!' I heard Harry shout but I felt a sharp butt on my behind and the goat was there, prodding me with her horns. She more or less pushed me through the gap in the wire and then the soldier was on us. 'Bloody kids!' he shouted, grabbing at me and missing. Then we were running down the lane, the soldier shouting after us. I saw the boy running ahead of us.

We'd just gone round a corner when there was a great explosion, clapping against my ears and knocking me down.

Chapter 3

It was all a bit mixed up after that but I tried to sort it out
as I wrote in my diary next day.

*Went to rescue Thomasina but a stupid boy was
chasing the goat and we nearly all got blown up when
the bomb went off. The soldier swore at us and we got
covered with mud and bits from the explosion. Harry's
goat butted the soldier and then Mum was there with her
curlers in and a policeman. Everyone was angry even
though we said it wasn't our fault and the boy ran off so
he never got into trouble and it wasn't fair. Harry went
off with the goat to stop her butting everyone. The bad
thing is that our cottage and Nurse Robin's will need a
lot of rebuilding and I got an angry telling-off from
Mum. The good thing is that we've got Thomasina at the
Sow and Pigs shut in our room in case she strays. Mrs
J. doesn't like us having a dirt tray there for her and I
think Joshua and Josephine Pie will be nervous.*

When the Army had taken the remains of the bomb
away we went with Nurse Robin and the village
policeman, PC Thorogood, to see what was left of our
belongings, picking our way between the bricks, glass
and earth thrown up by the explosion.

Nurse Robin's cottage had part of the front blown in

but the roof was still on. A blackbird sang in the garden, sitting on a broken tree and the sun shone brightly as if nothing at all had happened.

'I've got to get my uniform,' Nurse Robin cried, dodging the bomb crater and leaping inside her cottage before the policeman could stop her. While he was distracted, Mum and I went to look at Rose Cottage. The glass was blown out of the windows and about half the front wall was blown in. It looked very odd. My pink eiderdown was hanging down and the books I'd propped on the windowsill were on the ground with my old teddy, Rupert. You could see all our sitting room, like the stage-set in a panto – with pictures and ornaments smashed on the floor and dust everywhere. Mum picked her way through the rubble and came back with her precious little wireless and a cracked glass frame with her wedding photo – my tall, good-looking father beside small pretty Mum.

'Hey! You can't go inside. We'll have to get a builder to see how safe it is first!' the policeman shouted. Nurse Robin came round the side of her cottage, pushing her undamaged bike with a bag in the front basket. 'Bike's OK. Can't wait. Young Chrissie Rust is having her first baby.' She cycled off, her thin bird-legs pedalling like mad.

'You have to admire her,' Mum said as PC Thorogood, sweating in his uniform, made us come back to the pub.

'Looks like you'll not go back there for a while,' he said. 'Takes time these days to find a builder. A lot have gone off to the war.'

'And we've not been there long,' I said gloomily. I'd liked the roses in the garden and watching the birds.

'Well, the cottage was damp,' Mum said. 'And I'd rather have an inside lavatory. We'll look for something else.'

'But Mrs Jarvis won't want us to stay at the pub. She hates the mice,' I said.

Then I saw a pony and cart waiting outside the pub. It looked like the same grey pony Harry had ridden.

Harry jumped out, followed by a big, sun-tanned woman dressed in men's blue overalls and boots. Her black hair was in a fat pigtail, reaching her waist. She wore gold hoops in her ears and a red scarf at her neck. I wondered if she was a gypsy. 'I'm Harry's mum, Beatie Seddon,' she said. '*She's*' – I did a double-take – Harry was a girl! – 'in big trouble for going out to get our goat in the night and going near that bomb. When she came back last night she said the explosion must have damaged your cottage.'

Mum smiled. 'We certainly can't live there, until it's repaired.'

Mrs Seddon smiled back. 'We've got a spare bedroom. Not luxury but you're welcome to it.'

She had a funny way of talking, gruff and abrupt. I could see Mum was just going to refuse but at that moment Mrs Jarvis came to the pub door looking cross. Distantly, I heard Thomasina yowling. The mice wouldn't like the noise at all. Neither did Mrs Jarvis. 'Are you going to keep that cat in the room all day?' she asked.

'We're happy to have your cat too,' said Mrs Seddon.

'Let's go there,' I whispered to Mum. Harry was all right even if she didn't look like a girl. At least I'd have a friend at last and I might be allowed to ride a pony.

Mum smiled. 'Thank you very much. It will only be temporary, of course, while we look for somewhere else to live.'

Once Mum had made up her mind she acted quickly and in a moment, she'd paid Mrs Jarvis and thanked her, fetched her knitting bag, our gas masks and her small letter-case. I carried the mouse cage and Mrs Jarvis found a cardboard box for Thomasina. 'We'll have to fetch our clothes when they've propped up the front wall of the cottage,' Mum said and then we were off, clattering down the village street.

In front, Mum talked to Mrs Seddon, who answered with occasional grunts, looking straight ahead between the pony's ears.

'I'd like to kill that daft boy,' Harry muttered to me. 'I suppose he took our goat and then she got away from him.'

'I thought *you* were a boy,' I said.

Harry frowned and I thought I'd upset her. 'I wish I was. Don't want to wear dresses when I grow up and have silly perms and boyfriends. I've got an elder sister – then Dad wanted a boy to work on the farm. I think he was disappointed. But I'm just as strong as a boy.'

We had gone through the village and the pony was pulling us up a very rutty track towards an assortment of old sheds with rusting, corrugated iron roofs. Three more ponies came galloping up the field beside us.

'Oh, I love the little one!' I said.

'That's Tiny, the Shetland. Very obstinate. Bet she'd buck you off,' Harry said. 'I used to ride her when I was small. I'm getting too big for this one, Silver, now but there's no money to buy me a horse.'

We stopped by a rickety gate, which Harry opened. Hens of all colours and sizes scuttled away as she led the pony into the mucky-looking yard. A huge pig was standing in a pen, its feet on the top bar of the gate, grunting a welcome. 'That's Bertha,' Harry said. 'She's expecting piglets. The other pigs are in the field.'

Bits of rusty farm machinery littered the yard. 'Hop out,' Mrs Seddon said, helping Mum down. I hopped and then stood still as a file of geese rushed at me, wings outstretched, honking wildly.

'They're my burglar alarm. Won't hurt you,' said Mrs Seddon.

Harry led the pony and cart to one of the tumbledown sheds built on three sides of the yard while Mrs Seddon took us to a very old stone house on the fourth side. Its mossy tiled roof sagged in the middle. A tall, thin man stood in the doorway, leaning on a stick. One arm ended in a bandaged stump just below the elbow. He wore a black patch over one eye which made him look a bit sinister, like a pirate.

Mrs Seddon introduced him as her husband Dick. 'Just got him back from hospital,' she added casually. 'He was wounded at Dunkirk.'

I was impressed. 'Were you rescued by a little boat?' Mum and I had heard the news on her wireless, about

20

the thousands of Allied soldiers who got stuck in France as the Germans advanced, and masses of people from England sailed in boats of all sizes to rescue the ones who couldn't get on military boats.

Harry nudged me with a sharp elbow. 'He doesn't like to talk about it,' she hissed.

He'd not heard me, anyway. Mrs Seddon was explaining about Mum and me being sort of bombed out. He stared at us vaguely as if he was thinking of something else.

Then he smiled, and his face looked younger. 'Welcome to Hogsty Farm. We're not very grand here, mind.' He looked at the mouse cage where Josephine Pie was running up and down distractedly. 'Mice!' He sounded scornful. 'We've got enough of those – and rats.' Then he went inside the house.

'Gets black moods since he was wounded,' said Mrs Seddon. 'He saw so many friends killed – and ordinary French people too. The newsreel made out that the evacuation was a success but he says thousands died or were taken prisoner.'

We walked over the stone-flagged hall. I was carrying Thomasina's basket and saw the drips coming out of the bottom. 'She's weed.' I felt embarrassed.

Mrs Seddon laughed. 'She'd better get outside with our cats.'

'How many?' I asked.

'About six or so. They live in the hay-barn to keep the rats down.'

I knew they'd gang up against Thomasina, the new girl, and decided not to let her out yet.

We had chipped tin mugs of tea in the kitchen. Something nasty was boiling away on the old black range.

A hen fluttered out of the open back door. The kitchen table was laden with old newspapers, mugs, muddy-looking vegetables and a big bowl of dirt-smeared eggs.

'Pigswill's a bit pongy, Mum,' Harry said as she came in.

'Is it?' Mrs Seddon looked surprised and poked at the heaving mixture on the range with a wooden spoon. 'I've been so busy now it's haymaking I don't notice things.' She gulped down the last of her tea. 'You don't mind sleeping outside?'

Mum looked surprised and I thought of camping in a tent, which would have been fun – but Mrs Seddon showed us out of the back door through a flutter of hens. 'Mind the goose droppings,' she said, too late.

'And mind the broken step,' she said leading the way out of the yard gate into a field to a weather-boarded wooden hut. We followed her inside. The sun shone through the one closed window and it was baking hot. There was a cupboard, a bed, a chair, a jug and basin on a table, an old rug on the wooden floor and rows of books on long planks propped on bricks. 'Mel's room,' she said, opening the window a little way.

'Your…?' Mum began.

'My elder sister,' Harry said. 'We don't talk about her in front of Dad.'

'He's not himself. He's in pain, Harry,' Mrs Seddon said. 'Melanie's a Quaker and so she doesn't believe in fighting. But she's off in a military hospital, nursing.

22

Dad doesn't hold with God or the Quakers.'

It all sounded very complicated and I wondered what a Quaker was. I thought it might be something to do with the Quaker Oats Mum used to make porridge. She said it was good for me, which made me hate it all the more.

I put the mouse cage on a box in the corner and took poor Thomasina out of her basket. Her tail lashed as she sniffed round the room. Then she leaped on top of the cupboard.

'She'd be better outside but while she settles we can fix an earth tray and you can fetch her some of Auntie's milk,' Mrs Seddon said. 'There's candles and one oil lamp and once a week there's the tin bath in the kitchen. And we've an outside lavatory attached to our coalhouse.'

I'd so hoped for a proper inside lavatory and bathroom. I wanted to go right now so Harry showed me the way. Spider's webs hung thickly on the ceiling. The wooden seat was cracked and the lav smelled of tarred roads. At Rose Cottage Mum used to cut up the last of our paper bags but here there were only scratchy squares of newspaper hanging from a string on the door. It was a place you wanted to leave as soon as possible.

Harry was waiting for me outside. 'They're in the kitchen talking boring stuff about ration books and towels,' she said. 'I'm going to milk Auntie.' She didn't ask me to come but I followed her past a wired-off kitchen garden, with neat rows of vegetables, to a fenced field. At one side, there was a row of ancient-looking stone pigsties. Gaps in the stones were filled by more rusty corrugated iron and what looked like old wooden doors.

Harry walked off to where the white goat was tethered on a long chain at the far end of the field, which was overlooked by dark woods.

I stopped to watch a sow and two pink piglets who were quickly turning into brown piglets as they sprang about, squealing, at the muddy end of the run. 'Aren't they wonderful!' I said.

Harry looked back. 'Doesn't do to get fond of them,' she snapped. 'They'll be gone to market as soon as they're big enough. I reared a weakling piglet once and he followed me about all over the place but he had to go in the end. I was sad.'

I didn't feel so happy about eating my ration of two slices of bacon a week.

As I caught up with Harry the white goat looked at me, her head on one side and her slanting golden eyes watchful. Then she galloped towards us, her head down, horns at the ready.

'Watch it!' Harry shouted and I jumped, just in time.

Harry seized the chain. 'Bad girl, Auntie,' she said.

The goat stood quite still, looking as gentle as the goats in one of my favourite books, *Heidi*. 'Auntie doesn't like strangers,' Harry said. 'I can't see how that flipping boy managed to undo the chain and get her to come with him. I'm bloody well going to find where he lives and tell him off big and strong. Maybe he took Auntie to his home, first. He'd probably go through the gate at the top of the field and there might be tracks or something in the woods, leading to his home. I've a good mind to have a look when I've finished milking.'

'Can I come too?' I asked although I didn't think she'd find him, just following tracks, because he mightn't have gone home before Auntie got loose and invaded our garden. I guessed Harry would have slammed me down if I said that, though.

She frowned. 'There's the henhouse to clean out first, when I've finished milking.'

'I'll help.'

We walked to one of the sheds where Harry tied up Auntie, washed her hands rather vaguely under a cold tap, sat on a small box and began to milk the goat. Auntie was tied up to a ring in the wall. I leaned against the wall and watched the milk spurting between Harry's fingers.

'I'd like to try milking,' I said.

Harry frowned. 'I know you townees – you'll trot round doing little bits but never getting your hands dirty.'

I was cross. 'I'm not like that. Give me something nasty to do and I'll show you!'

'OK. I will. See, there's a lot to do here now Mel's away and Dad's – well, crippled.' She emphasised the word unnecessarily. 'Someone's got to help Mum with the animals and the vegetables. She's got her hands full looking after Dad. Nurse Robinson comes in every day to put new dressings on.' She hesitated. 'And Dad's gone a bit funny. Gets angry at the least thing or sits around not talking and sometimes . . . ' She turned away, her head pressed into Auntie's flank so I could only see her short, spiky hair. 'Sometimes he cries. Mum doesn't know I've seen him.' She stopped milking and turned round. 'Promise you won't say anything to anyone, cut your throat and hope to die.'

'I promise.' I thought it must be awful to see a man cry. I'd seen Mum cry once, last year when we were still in London, living high above the city.

The war had just started. Home on leave, Dad had put up some blackout curtains on the windows in our top floor flat on Highgate Hill. The curtains fell down and the air-raid warden came round, complaining that our light was shining all over London. Somehow it led to Mum and Dad arguing in fiercely quiet voices and I don't think it was about blackout. I carried Thomasina down all the stairs to the patch of garden below for her daily exercise and when I got back, Mum was crying but she wouldn't say why. She said Dad had gone back to his RAF station, so I thought she was crying because she missed him. Now I wasn't sure I was right.

'It'll be different when my dad gets better,' Harry said in a more cheerful voice. 'He'll probably be like Captain Hook, you know, with a hook on the end of his arm.' She swore – words I'd not heard before – as Auntie kicked at the bucket and some of the milk splashed out.

I thought about school. We'd arrived in term-time but Mum had said we'd get used to the place first and I would start in September. 'Where do you go to school?'

'Miles away, by bus to Felford. Ancient teachers – most of the young ones are in the war – horribly strict and boring but luckily we sometimes get an air raid so we go into the shelter. That makes a change. I'm no book-swat like Mel. She wants to go to University.'

She picked up the bucket and wiped her hands on her overalls. 'If you clean the henhouse I'll clean the tack and then we can go. Might take the ponies. Can you ride?'

'Sort of.' I didn't want to put her off by explaining I'd only once been led along on a pony long ago at some half-forgotten trip to a zoo. Also, I didn't know what 'tack' was but I wasn't going to ask.

Harry gave me a bucket of water and a long-handled brush. The henhouse was boiling hot and smelly and I hated every minute of cleaning it. Give me mice any time – they make smaller poos. To make it worse, the geese had followed me and I heard them honking crossly outside, ready to ambush me.

When I'd finished the nasty job, I came out, dealt with the geese by banging my brush against the bucket to scare them off and found Harry in the yard, cleaning saddles and the cart harness. Two skinny tabby cats slunk across the yard and disappeared into a collapsing barn. I heard a screech as they fought. I worried about Thomasina. It might have been better if she'd been a male cat, as we'd thought when we named her Thomas. Then the vet said we'd got it wrong.

When I said I'd finished Harry didn't thank me but said her mother had some bread and cheese ready for lunch. Then we could go out.

27

In the kitchen, Mum smiled at me. 'Making friends, Pipkin? I've left an earth tray and food for Thomasina. And isn't Mrs Seddon kind to lend me these?' She smoothed down a man's shirt. The corduroy trousers were too big and had holes at the knees. Anyone would have thought she'd got the most marvellous outfit!

Dick Seddon sat without speaking, very slowly nibbling at a cheese sandwich. He looked as if he didn't know we were there.

Harry and I ate quickly, the usual wartime grey bread, strange-tasting goat's cheese and apples. I thought wistfully of the oranges and bananas you couldn't get now. They seemed to belong to another world. Mrs Seddon poured us out glasses of goat's milk. Mine tasted funny but I was thirsty so I drank it.

'I want to return Mrs Jarvis's dress and buy toothpaste and things from the shop,' Mum said. 'And find out if there's anything to let in the village. I wonder how soon we can get our clothes out of the cottage.'

'If they're waiting for someone to make the walls safe, it'll take a few days. Hogsty End moves slowly at the best of times,' Mrs Seddon said. 'Try the Vicarage. The Vicar might know of something.'

'He's a dead loss.' Dick Seddon spat out the words

'Now, Dick. That's no way to talk. He's given you plenty of his time,' Mrs Seddon said reprovingly.

'Old fool! Doesn't know when to go, that's his problem. Always wanting to pray. As if that does any good. And what's he know about fighting a war?'

Nobody talked after that.

As soon as we'd finished, Harry nodded at me and got up. At home I had to ask to leave the table but here it was different.

'I ought to tell Mum we're going out and fetch my gas mask,' I said as Harry led the way to the pony field, armed with bits of cut-up apples and carrots in a bucket.

She looked surprised. 'Why? As long as I do my work round here, Mum never worries. And we never bother with gas masks here except when I go to school.' She sounded scornful and I wasn't sure if I really liked her, after all.

She banged on the bucket and the ponies came galloping straight at us. I've always wanted to be brave so I shut my eyes and didn't move, expecting at any moment to be pushed over.

Harry giggled. 'Got a fly in your eye?'

A whiskery nose nudged my face. I opened my eyes. The pony looked at me, then went to join the others, pushing to get near the bucket. 'You'd better have old Bracken. He's half Suffolk Punch and half Dartmoor,' she said, hanging on to the halter of a sturdy pony with a reddish-brown coat, curiously speckled with white. 'You're much too tall for the little 'uns. Here, hang on to him.' She had no trouble catching Silver, slipping a bridle over his halter and swinging easily onto his back. 'Let's ride bareback,' she said clipping her heels into the pony's sides. 'You've done that?'

I'd never heard of it and wondered for a moment if I had to take my shirt off but I realised we weren't to have saddles. I made a sort of grunting sound as we took the

29

ponies into the yard and my voice was drowned by the whinnying of the ponies left behind.

She pointed at a long-legged pale gold pony with a frisky look. 'Mum will train Goldie later on when she's not so busy. Then she'll sell her.' She slipped off Silver and put the bridle on Bracken. 'Before Dad came back, she took out a few kids for lessons but she's no time now.'

I tried to throw myself on as she did but kept sliding back and then I yelled as Bracken nipped my behind!

Harry laughed. 'He always does that if you mess about. It usually doesn't leave a mark,' she said, getting off and giving me a leg up. My feet dangled below the pony's belly but the ground was still too far away. I liked the horse smell, though, and gave Bracken a pat to show I had no hard feelings.

Harry was looking at me critically. 'Sit up. You look like a sack of potatoes. Are you sure you've ridden much before? You're not holding the reins properly. Try like this.' She unclasped my fingers and pushed them into position. Her hands were hard, with dirty broken nails.

I was afraid she'd call the ride off so I said, 'Just out of practice.'

Then Bracken followed Harry's pony out of the yard and up the field, past the pigsties and Auntie, who ran to the end of her chain and pawed the ground, head lowered.

The ponies probably knew they were out of the goat's range and went on. Bracken had a long ginger mane and I clutched at it as he trotted to catch up. I felt as if my teeth were rattling in my head.

Harry was inspecting the gate which was done up with a bit of wire. 'It's been undone and twisted a different way. Dad said I couldn't have chained her up properly. Just shows we shouldn't leave Auntie out at night even when it's warm like this. After all, goats are very useful in wartime. She could easily be goat-napped. I expect the boy wanted her for her milk. Probably his parents sent him out to get her.'

I wondered how you could hide someone else's goat in a small village but I supposed they might have planned a get-away in a van – if they had enough petrol.

We walked the ponies down a narrow, twisting track between thick bushes until we came to a clearing where the path divided.

'You might help me look for tracks,' Harry said crossly. She'd dismounted and was peering at the dirt and dead leaves that covered the paths. 'Ah! I can see goat droppings this way and little hoof-marks,' she said, leaping on again.

She took the right-hand fork and we rode through trees and tall bracken.

Again the ponies trotted and I hung on, somehow, glad Harry wasn't looking back. Maybe riding was easier with a saddle. At least Bracken was keen to follow Silver.

Clouds of flies followed us and I was so busy swatting them off my face and hands that I didn't notice Silver had gone out of sight, through a thick grove of fir trees.

I suddenly felt lost and kicked at Bracken's sides to catch up. Then I wished I hadn't as he broke into a canter and I only stayed on by hanging round his neck.

I found Silver standing while Harry looked down into a wooded valley. 'I've never gone down there before,' she said. 'It's sort of dark and bad-feeling. Besides, it's quite a way from home. Before the war, this part of the woods was marked off as private for shooting for the Manor House. Why are you hanging on to Bracken's mane like that? I bet you can't ride at all!'

It was her voice, sharp and nasty, that goaded me on. I don't know why, but I wanted to show I wasn't just a feeble townee. I kicked at Bracken's sides and loosened my tight grip on the reins and he shot off, along the path into the darkest part of the wood. He was galloping! I clung on, lying almost flat on his neck, holding on to his mane. The path was narrow so bushes scraped my face and I saw we were going under a low branch. I lay even flatter and we thundered on. Faintly behind me I heard Harry shout as we plunged downwards. I nearly slid down the pony's neck but managed to cling on.

I heard Silver's hooves behind me, thudding softly on the pine needles. 'Stop him!' shouted Harry. 'Hang on to the reins, you bloody idiot!'

Then there was a gunshot, quite near. Bracken stopped so suddenly that I catapulted over his head and landed in a prickly bush.

I was so scratched it was hard not to yell as Harry helped me scramble out, while trying to hold both ponies at the same time. 'Idiot! Stupid bloody idiot!' she muttered which made me so cross I forgot the scratches.

I was standing, dazed, picking bits of twig out of my

32

hair, when another gunshot rang out and big black birds rose out of the trees, wildly cawing. The sound of the gunshot seemed to echo through the woods and set off a dog barking somewhere, deep and fierce.

'It might be a German parachutist with a gun!' I hissed, crouching. We'd heard stories of Germans disguised as nuns or tramps who could be dropped from a plane to spy out the land ready for invasion. I had giggled a bit in the past, thinking of nuns floating down from the sky – their long clothes blown up to show their knickers!

'Don't talk soft.' Harry hooked both ponies up to a tree, then pushed through the bushes. 'There's a little cottage down there and someone's got a rifle pointing out of the window!' she whispered.

I joined her. Below us, in a little valley surrounded by thick trees, was a cottage whose tiled roof was smothered with thick ivy. A trickle of smoke came out of the chimney. Washing hung on a line and hens scratched the ground. A big golden dog was chained to a kennel at the side of the cottage.

Then I saw the glint of a rifle pointing through an upstairs window.

Chapter 4

My heart literally thudded against my ribs as I wondered how far a bullet could go. A grey-haired woman pushed through the washing and hurried to the front door, calling something we couldn't hear. At the same time a boy ran out of the cottage carrying something. He ran to undo the dog's chain. I had time to see he had almost white hair before he disappeared down the track that led from the cottage.

'I bet that's him!' I said.

'I'm going after him,' Harry said angrily.

'But you might get shot...' I began then the gun jerked back from the window.

'They're probably shooting at a fox,' she said, unhitching the ponies' bridles. 'Come on, I'll give you a leg up. I'm going to catch that boy.'

I didn't want to show I was scared of the gun, so I let her heave me on and the ponies walked down the narrow path into the valley. Something brushed my cheek and I screamed.

'Shut up!' Harry said. 'We don't want them coming out with that gun.'

I looked back. A bird's bleached skeleton hung from a branch. Then I saw another. 'Look!' I pointed. 'It's horrible.'

Harry looked over her shoulder. 'That's nothing.

Gamekeepers shoot vermin – magpies, jackdaws, rats and so on and hang them from bushes. It's supposed to warn off other vermin who might attack the pheasants.'

We'd come to the bottom now. The trees had thinned out and we could see the cottage through a gap. It looked blind and strange with the windows closed and the curtains drawn.

'Funny, drawing the curtains in broad daylight,' Harry said.

'It looks kind of secret,' I said. 'Sinister. I'd not like to live there.'

'Come on – we've got to find that boy and tell him off,' and she was urging Silver along the track, after him.

I thought we hadn't a hope of catching him but I hung on to Bracken and caught up with Harry. We turned a corner and saw the boy ahead with the golden dog at his side. He turned, saw us and ran into the bushes at the side of the track.

Harry jumped off and flung Silver's reins at me. 'Hold her,' she said in her bossy way.

There was a great barking and growling and crashing in the bushes and then Harry came back, pulling the boy along with one hand and holding the dog's collar with the other.

'Let me go!' the boy cried, trying to get away but he was small with starvation-thin arms and legs and Harry was all muscle. The ponies pricked their ears and looked cautiously at the dog.

'I'm not going back,' the boy said. 'I hate them!' Sweat ran down his pale face and he muttered, 'Gotta stitch,' clutching his side.

He was odd-looking with eyelashes as white as his hair. He reminded me of my white mouse, Joshua, and I half expected him to have red eyes but they were a very pale blue. He was wearing clothes a size too big for him, long shorts and a ripped shirt hanging out of his waistband and he clutched an old-looking black leather bag like a lifeline.

I suddenly felt sorry for him. 'We won't take you back,' I promised recklessly as he folded up on the ground, looking exhausted.

Harry stood over him, hands on her hips, thrusting her head forward, saying, 'I want to know why you took our goat.'

The boy looked up at us and tears fell down his face. 'I don't like creatures tied up and I wanted company,' he said. 'But she pulled the rope out of my hands so I followed her as fast as I could, right through the woods to the cottages. Then I saw that hole and went to see what it was. When the soldier shouted I ran away.' He blinked his white eyelashes and swallowed before going on: 'Then there was that awful bang and stuff flying in the air just like . . . ' He stopped and began to shake as if he were cold.

'Acting up,' Harry whispered to me but I couldn't bear to see it. I sat beside him in the shade and put my arm round him, yes, actually put my arm round a boy! It's not something I'm in the habit of doing. The boys I knew seemed to shout and fight a lot and I've always avoided them. But this boy was like a frightened animal.

For a moment he leaned against me, still shaking. Then he probably felt silly so he struggled away. 'Got anywhere

36

I could hide from Them?' he asked in a whisper.

'Are you an evacuee?' Harry asked.

'Sort of. The Smiths are kind of relations and I hate them because they're Germans. They pretend to be called Smith.'

I know Harry was thinking the same as me. He was making things up.

'Do they beat you?' I asked, looking at his legs for bruises but they were so dirty it was hard to see.

'I dodge off before *he* can get me. He's going batty and she's always on at me.'

'Where are your parents?' Harry asked.

'My dad's abroad – somewhere. Mum didn't say but I think he's a spy working for the British,' he said proudly. 'Mum and me'd gone from London to Gran's. Hit-and-run plane got Gran's house. Gran was killed.' He paused. 'My mum's in hospital.' His whispering voice died away.

'Where was that?' Harry asked. I could tell she still didn't believe him.

He sniffed loudly. 'Gran's house was on the East coast and those stinking Germans were only half an hour across the sea by air. I hate them!' The boy's voice was fierce now. 'A plane bombed the house when I was out birdwatching. I should've been there. Got back to find a stinking heap of rubble instead of a home, didn't I?'

'Will your mum get better?' Harry asked.

He wiped the tears off his face with the back of a dirty hand. 'Yeah. 'Course she will. So I need to be there for her, not here with these German spies.' The dog licked his face and he hugged it fiercely.

Then he stiffened as we heard someone calling. The woman's voice grew nearer. 'Max, Max! Come back!' The dog pricked his ears and whined.

'They want their dog.'

'No, they're calling me. I'm Max. The dog's Winston after Mr Churchill.' The voice drew nearer but I couldn't see anyone yet. 'Come on, please hide me.' He clutched at Harry's arm with dirty fingers. 'He's got a gun and I think they're both spies!' He wasn't whispering now.

'We'll help you escape! You'll have to ride in front of me,' Harry said, seizing Max and putting him on Silver.

He looked dazed but not scared as she mounted the pony and held him in front of her. He was still clutching the leather bag. I had to mount Bracken on my own but I managed it better this time.

I looked down and saw the dog peacefully loping beside us; he seemed in no hurry to go home. Maybe Max's relations were horrible to him, too.

'Where are we going?' I shouted, my voice jerking as I bounced on the pony's back, somehow staying on. I just knew how scornful Harry would be if I fell off.

'I know a place he can hide,' she shouted back. 'But I don't know this part of the wood or where this track comes out.'

We rounded the corner. The sun shone on a tarmac road. There was a signpost but it was blacked out so German parachutists couldn't find their way about.

I could see over the hedge across the road. Girls in dungarees were stacking sheaves of what must be corn into pointed stacks. A carthorse plodded along with some sort of cutting machine led by two boys.

Harry saw them. 'That's the Wilsons' field. And I know Spike Wilson who's leading the horse. I guess the other boy's the evacuee they were expecting from London. Spike and me's always fighting. If he sees us he'll tell.'

She quickly turned Silver to the right, to a path that went almost parallel to the one we'd come down. 'The trouble is, Mel's den – as she called it – is fairly near our house,' she muttered.

First of all we were on a woodland track and then Harry turned again into a narrow path running between lumps of rock smothered with moss and ferns. It was in the shade but seemed to trap the heat and flies. Bracken's neck was frothy with sweat and Max kept saying he was thirsty.

Bracken followed Silver through a narrow break in the rocks.

'Right – we're here,' Harry said, dismounting. She reached out to help Max but he muttered irritably, 'I can do it,' and slithered after her. Again she tied the ponies up to a thin sapling where they stood, tossing their heads against the flies.

Branches were stacked against a stony bank.

'This was Mel's hide – for birdwatching,' Harry said. 'Sometimes she let me come along too but she said I made too much noise.'

Max was wiping the sweat off his face but he stopped and grinned. 'That's terrific! I know lots about birds.'

Harry ducked into a kind of side opening. 'Come on,' she said.

Max pushed past me eagerly, followed by Winston.

It was dark inside and smelled musty. 'Can't see nothing,' Max said. 'Smells of rotting things and old socks.'

My eyes got used to the dim light filtering through the opening and I saw that we were at the entrance to a small cave. There was a hole in the branches, letting in a strip of light.

'Mel used to look through that hole with her binocs,' Harry said. 'She saw badgers and foxes.'

'Do they bite?' Max asked nervously. 'There weren't no badgers at Lowestoft.'

'Not unless you try to catch them,' Harry said. She went into the shallow cave. 'Yes, she left the blankets here and the biscuit tin. Something for you to eat,' she told Max.

She opened the rusty tin by the gap of light. There was a greenish mass of crumbs inside. Max sniffed. 'Ugh! Them biscuits are wriggling!'

'We'll bring you food and candles,' Harry said.

'I just want to go home,' Max said. 'I got some money plus what I pinched from Them but I guess it isn't enough.' He opened the bag and shook out a stream of coins. He muttered to himself as he counted it. 'This is my gran's old bag. All they found of her. Half a crown, three bob, a sixpence and four pennies. Probably not enough. It's a long way from here.' He put the money back and I saw the gleam of something that looked like a photograph in a frame.

I was a bit shocked. 'You took your cousins' money?'

'My gran had half a crown in there already. And the Smiths only had that money I could find. After all, they owe me for all the work I've done. Pumping water from the well mornings, filling the copper for Her washing, looking for eggs, fetching shopping, scrubbing kitchen floor. Slave labour, it was!' He took a breath and then ran on at speed. 'And that dotty old man saying he'd give me the strap if I didn't stop whingeing.'

'So he didn't actually beat you,' Harry said.

'Not exactly. She says he's got something called shell shock from the last war but I reckon he's just gone potty.'

'War makes some people go funny,' Harry said thoughtfully.

'You said the cousins were German. Smith doesn't sound a German name,' I said. It was going to be difficult, I could see, keeping him here and if he was just spinning a tale . . . whatever shell shock was it sounded a bit phoney.

'I'll die of thirst if you don't get me a drink,' he whispered. 'And I saw their name on a letter – it's spelled SCHMIDT. They call themselves Smith so they won't get put in prison.' He sounded very sure of himself. 'And they call each other by foreign names, Ulla and Hans – I bet they don't tell anyone else those names.'

'Foreign names,' Harry said thoughtfully. 'And it's funny that your mother sent you to stay with German spies. You'd think she'd know more about them.'

He shot up to her and raised his skinny arm, fist clenched. 'Don't you say anything against my mum! They're related to my dad and he fixed it up before he went away. He reckoned those bombers would come. Mum never met them but Mrs Smith said I could have their son's room now he'd joined the Army and Mum could sleep on a couch. We shouldn't have waited so long. Well,

41

after . . . the bomb . . . a neighbour put me on the train with a label on me – a label just like a kid! Then Mrs Smith met me in London, at the station. The son's a gamekeeper and Winston's his dog. The Smiths are sort of evacuees too, they *say* from London, a few months back. And now they're living near that big secret house.'

'You mean Cotefield Manor, I suppose,' Harry said. 'I did hear there were government people from London billeted there, doing war-work.'

'She – Mrs Smith – works there, cleaning. I bet she spies on them. And she leaves me with that mad old man. He gets his gun out as soon as she's gone. He nearly shot the postman.'

'You'd think the police would be after them,' Harry said.

'The village bobby came on his bike but she was nice as pie to him and gave him tea and a piece of cake and the old man acted quite normal, just sitting quiet in his rocking chair. They're clever, see. And they don't let poor Winston in the house.'

I felt the dog's tail thump against my leg as he heard his name. 'If we keep him here we'll have to find dog-food,' Harry said. 'It's not going to be easy with rationing. Hadn't we better let him loose so he goes back?'

Max sat down and put his arm round Winston. 'I gotta have him. My dog Joey was killed in the raid, too. I HATE those bloody Germans and I wish I was older so I could go out and kill them all!' His voice had risen to a shout. Winston got up and ran round the cave, sniffing and growling, looking for Bad People.

Harry and I just stood there. Max's war was different

42

from mine. I didn't like new schools and moving but Max had lost his gran, his home, his dog and now his mum was in hospital.

Harry broke the silence. 'Our dog got run over last month by an Army lorry. So I know how you feel. We'd better go. I've got to shut up the hens. We'll get food and drink to you somehow and more money so you can go home.'

'Thanks.' He collapsed onto the pile of blankets and Winston went to lie beside him. 'These don't half smell mouldy,' he complained. 'I don't like it here.'

'Won't hurt you,' Harry said briskly. 'You're lucky to find somewhere to hide.'

Max was like that. One minute you felt sorry for him, the next he whined about things and you wished you'd never got involved.

'It'll be fun. You can live on blackberries and nuts,' I said, remembering one of my Enid Blyton books.

'He can't. They're not ripe yet,' Harry snapped. 'Nothing to eat in the woods unless you can trap a rabbit or pheasant. We'll get you food.'

As we went I heard him say, 'Don't leave me alone.'

But we had to.

Chapter 5

'Thank goodness you're all right!' Mum was waiting by the farmyard gate and rushed at me. I saw Harry smile and felt horribly embarrassed.

'Of course I am,' I said, ducking out of Mum's arms.

'I'm sure you never told Harriet you'd not been on a pony before.'

Harry laughed. 'I guessed. She'll be stiff as anything tomorrow.'

Mrs Seddon joined us. 'Your dad's been asking for you, Harry. You're late for tea and you know how he hates that. And there's the hens to shut up and those ponies could do with a rub down.'

'OK, OK,' Harry said crossly and I wondered how we'd get back to Max.

'Very thoughtless of you, Pippa,' Mum said – as if it was all my fault! It was so unfair of her. She'd be surprised if she knew we'd been rescuing a boy from German spies. 'Come in as quickly as you can,' she added.

We rubbed down the ponies and let them loose. They immediately went to drink from an old tin bath full of water in their field. Harry put her head under the tap feeding the bath and I copied her, wringing out my wet plaits afterwards like dishcloths.

That was all wrong too. 'What have you done to your

hair, Pip?' Mum exclaimed as we came into the kitchen.

Mr Seddon was tearing a piece of bread into little bits. 'Never do that again, Harry, just going off when there's work to be done.' He put the bits of bread round his plate in a kind of pattern.

We had what I thought was chicken stew with potatoes and beans. I'm not a great eater and the kitchen was hot; it was worse when Mrs Seddon said, 'Harry shot that rabbit yesterday, Dick. Getting a really good eye, now.'

His good hand shook as he lifted a spoonful of stew to his mouth. 'Good thing as I'm not likely to use a gun again.'

I pushed pieces of rabbit to the edge of my plate and then into my hankie when nobody was looking.

Mum said, 'Well, the Vicar's found me someone to prop up the front of our cottage in a day or two – rebuilding's going to take much longer – and his wife's roped me in to sew curtains when I'm not working at the canteen on Boar's Hill.'

'Curtains?' asked Mrs Seddon.

'I heard at the shop – curtains for Wellington bombers,' I said excitedly. 'Just think, Mum, Dad's bomber might gets your curtains! What colours will you choose?'

Mum laughed. 'They're blackout curtains, so nobody can see the bombers coming.'

'This canteen work too. I suppose it's that camouflaged barn on the hill – it's a long way to walk,' Mrs Seddon said.

Mum smiled. 'I can cope with that. Apparently the canteen's for soldiers and airmen billeted nearby. There's a few French Canadians, too, and I can speak French quite well. But maybe I won't begin till Pippa starts school. It wouldn't be fair to leave her on her own.'

Harry winked at me. 'She won't be on her own here, will she, Mum? There's lots she can do to help me.'

Mum looked at me doubtfully.

'Yes – I'd like that,' I said.

'I went to the cottage as well,' she went on. 'My poor cabbages and carrots were dying of thirst. And I fetched a few everyday clothes.'

'Was it safe to do that?' I asked. My mother often did things that were a bit risky, like walking at the edge of cliff paths. She always said I forgot she was still quite young. What she didn't know was that ever since the war began I was scared she'd get ill or even die. I felt unsafe, as if the ground might open under my feet. Maybe I was right. After all, Max had lost his home in an instant.

Mr Seddon had been silently hunched over the table, not really listening. He looked up. 'Don't forget those hens, Harry. I saw a fox in the field the other day. And there's the watering. The ground's dry as dust at the moment.'

'I won't forget, Dad,' Harry said. 'Is it OK if Pip and me go for another ride when I've done the work? She's getting on so well.'

'That Bracken's as safe as houses,' Mrs Seddon said. 'I put my beginners on him.'

'Please, Mum,' I said, although I was aching already from riding.

'If you promise to get home well before dark. And of

46

course hurry back if the siren goes.' I nodded. Then Mum said she wanted to help as the Seddons had been so kind, putting us up, so she washed the dishes while I went to see how Thomasina was.

As soon as I opened the door, our cat rushed out and ran towards the farmhouse. I ran after her, calling, but I needn't have bothered as she ran back, a tabby cat in hot pursuit.

I stood, helpless, as both cats disappeared over the field and into the wood.

I put my bits of left-over rabbit on the step to lure Thomasina back. Then I checked on the mice and gave them their food. Joshua, whiskers twitching, was looking anxiously out of the little door from their bedroom but Josephine Pie ran to the side of the cage, hoping to be let out for tightrope practice. 'Later,' I told her.

I found Harry watering a row of lettuces. 'Your cat's going to murder Thomasina,' I told her.

She grinned at me. 'I saw them. She certainly can run even though she's fat! I think you're too soft with her. She'll come back, you'll see.'

Harry just didn't understand because she'd lived in one place all the time. Poor Thomasina was all mixed up.

But it was my problem, not Harry's. And there was the boy to help. 'Hadn't we better go to Max soon?' I thought of the scraggy boy, crouched in the cave, thirsty and hungry.

'Got to finish this first,' Harry said. 'The veg will die in this heatwave if I don't water them.'

I said I'd help her. 'What'll we take him, anyway?' I asked as I walked up and down the rows.

'Keep your voice down!' Harry whispered. 'Mum's just come out to feed the pigs. I'm going to nip in and find what I can in the larder. Meet you in the henhouse.'

I finished the watering and Mrs Seddon thanked me. 'I'm just going to get Auntie in for the night – we can't risk her going off again. Where's Harry?'

'I think she's gone to the lavatory.' I didn't like lying to her.

I was really tired and aching now and I began to wonder if Max might have been lying all along. We could get in big trouble, hiding him.

Some of the hens had already begun to settle for the night and they clucked at me indignantly. 'Don't forget I cleaned your house,' I told them.

Harry came in with a knapsack under her arm. 'Mostly stale bread, apples and a bottle of water,' she said. 'Mum would notice if I took any of Auntie's cheese. And I've dog biscuits for Winston.'

'Supposing we get arrested for kidnapping?' I asked her. 'After all, Max might have made it all up – about them being unkind to him and being German spies.'

'I thought you were sorry for him!'

'I am.'

'Let's just give him this one meal and I've got nearly two pounds in small change, then he can get a ticket to his old home.'

'Did you pinch it?'

'No! I broke open my piggy-bank. Come on, we got

48

to get all the hens in.'

This took time as some of the hens were determined to roost in the hedge. Then it was the turn of the geese who lived in one of the yard sheds. I tried not to look scared as the biggest bird opened large wings, squawking at me.

Harry laughed. 'That's Nelson, our gander. He doesn't like strangers. Mum says he keeps off any burglars.' She waved her arms and he followed the others into the shed and she shut the door. 'Let's go,' she said.

We caught the ponies. I was so stiff Harry had to haul me onto Bracken. She slapped a battered hard hat on my head. It was too small and pinched round my forehead. 'You're not doing badly for a complete beginner,' she said as we started off up the field. 'Probably Mum will give you a lesson or two when Dad's feeling better.'

I called Thomasina but there was no sign of her. I just hoped that horrible tabby hadn't murdered her.

I suppose I was looking out for Thomasina and not really thinking about Max, so it was a shock when we approached the cave and heard loud sobbing and the words, 'I need you, Mum! I'll never see you again. Why did you go and get bombed? If you'd come with me you'd be all right,' as we got off and tied up the ponies. He obviously hadn't heard us coming.

We stood outside as Max went on sobbing and talking to himself. I knew Harry was thinking the same as me; Max wasn't acting a part and his mother wasn't in hospital, she was dead.

Winston rushed at us, barking. 'He'll give us away,'

Harry said, quickly bribing him with a bit of biscuit.

'I thought you'd forgotten me,' Max said in a wobbly voice.

Harry gave him the water in an old lemonade bottle and he drank eagerly. 'Some for Winston,' Harry said, taking it from him and pouring it into a tin bowl she'd brought. The dog was as thirsty as Max, who wasn't very grateful for the food. 'The bread's dry,' he grumbled.

'We heard you talking to yourself. Your mum's dead, isn't she?' Harry asked.

'No – she's just gone away.' His voice was desperate. 'They never found nothing but Gran's handbag. The house was on fire. Maybe she ran out in time. Maybe she's in hospital and nobody knows it's her... Maybe...'

'Is that why you want to go back? To look for her? To make sure?' I asked.

He looked out of the gap in the hide. 'There's a green woodpecker! It's in my bird book. I never seen one before.'

'Why go back?' I asked him.

'To make sure. Like you said. I suppose I thought I'd camp out in our shed. That's still there.'

'Didn't your father come back when your mum died?'

'I told you, stupid! He's in France or Germany – I don't know which. We've not heard. He doesn't know about her. You know the Nazis hate the Jews? I think he's helping Jews escape and spying as well.' He looked confused, perhaps again remembering his mum wasn't alive.

'Won't they send a telegram to your dad so he comes back?' I asked.

He looked at me scornfully. 'Don't be daft! Don't you hear the News? You think a nice kind Nazi is going to deliver a telegram to my dad wherever he's hiding? He'll not know about Mum dying for ages, probably. If he was here, I'd be OK. Dad would take me away and find somewhere to live. He's terribly brave and clever...' His voice died away.

'I don't think you can go home,' Harry said. 'The police would pick you up. Isn't there anyone else who'd have you?'

'No. Not now Gran's gone.' He gave a piece of bread to Winston.

'Didn't you say you came from London? Maybe you could stay with a friend there, in your road.'

'All the kids from my London school were evacuated. And they'd just send me back here, wouldn't they?' He slumped down on the floor. 'Help me get back. Mum might be somewhere,' he said between sobs.

I can't bear tears. I crouched down and patted his shoulder.

'We'd better go,' Harry said. 'It's sunset.' She gave the dog a handful of biscuits. 'Winston needs meat. We'll have to get him something.'

'Max – we'll think of a plan,' I promised wildly.

He buried his face in Winston's fur as we went out.

'We'd better use that money for food now,' Harry said, as we rode back. 'I mean, he can't go back.'

'But we can't keep him hidden for ever,' I said. 'Someone's bound to find out and then we'll be had up for kidnapping.'

'A real little ray of sunshine, aren't you? We'd better get a move on or there'll be trouble at home.' She dug her heels in Silver's sides and trotted ahead. I guessed it was because she didn't know what to do but I was so tired and hot that I couldn't argue. I'd even given up calling Thomasina. She was probably at this moment on her way back to Eastbourne.

She looked back. 'Don't lean forward and clutch his mane. You only rise to the trot when you've got a saddle. Just sit normally.'

I was feeling sad for Max and this made me even more cross with Harry so even when Bracken and I caught up with her, I didn't speak. The golden light of the setting sun threw long shadows across the path and at least it was a little cooler.

I tried to make a plan for Max. I had an idea but of course Harry squashed it as soon as we were walking the ponies through the gate. 'How about telling people the Smiths are spies and treat Max badly? Then he'll get taken away.'

'And go where?' she said. 'He'd just be put in an orphanage or something.'

At my last school, we'd read bits of *Oliver Twist* and wasn't there a terrible place called Dotheboys Hall, where the boys were half starved and beaten? I couldn't bear to think of poor Max somewhere like that. 'Couldn't your mum have him as an evacuee?'

'Not while Dad's in such a state.'

'Maybe we could when the cottage is repaired.'

'Anyway, I bet they won't believe us. We'd just get into big trouble and he'd get sent back,' she said. 'People never believe children.' Bats squeaked and flitted above us in the dusk as we walked down the field. I could see Mum, standing by the gate again. Harry would laugh at me.

But she didn't. She was still thinking of Max. 'His mum's obviously dead – he couldn't act that well, but we don't know if he's made it up about the Smiths just because he's homesick. Just imagine how you'd feel if your mum died and you were sent somewhere strange. You'd probably hate the new people, whatever they were like.'

'Probably.' I agreed and wished she'd not talked of mothers dying because it gave me that feeling again, that nothing was safe any more.

That night I wrote in my diary by the light of a candle. We'd lit the oil lamp in our room but its soft glow didn't reach the camp bed that Mrs Seddon had found for me. Harry had brought us a jug of hot water and we'd washed in the chipped china basin. Mum was sitting up in Mel's sagging bed, re-reading some of Dad's letters. By the light of the flickering candles her face was sad.

I wondered if her usually cheerful face was an act to reassure me.

I wrote: *I'm aching all over from riding but I shan't tell Harry because she's bossy enough without that. Tomorrow we're going to buy food at the shop and try to* think what do about Max. Mum doesn't seem very upset about Thomasina – she says she might have gone back to the cottage and we'll look tomorrow. I miss having her curled on my feet at night. The mice aren't the same. Mum says they smell and I have to clean the cage out tomorrow. When we got in Nurse Robin was there in the back room putting dressings on Mr Seddon's 'stump' – he's actually called Sergeant Seddon because he's still sort of in the Army. She calls him Sarge. I think he likes it. She had a cup of tea with us and said she'd talked to a builder and it would be more than a month before either of us could move back because he's short-handed. 'Remember there's a war on,' she said, like everyone else does ALL the time. Then she said she'd heard from the policeman's mother (who has something nasty wrong with her legs) that a boy staying with the Smiths was reported missing. I felt my face go red but Harry just asked polite questions. Nurse Robin twittered (she does) on about the poor boy having lost his mother and home and how nobody knew much about the Smiths except the postman said the old man had a gun and he'd seen a letter with Smith spelled in a German way and maybe they weren't the game-keeper's parents but traitors in disguise. So Harry whispered to me when she brought the water that Max probably was telling the truth. I can't write any more because I'm so tired and aching from riding.

Chapter 6

Harry said the owner of the village shop, where I'd been before, was called Edie Button. Now she leaned over the counter, her face glowing with excitement. Luckily, Harry's mum wanted a loaf of bread and a bag of porridge oats – yes, it was porridge for breakfast at the Seddons', I might have known it, just like home – so we had an excuse to go shopping for Max's food.

'Have you heard there's a boy missing?' Edie Button said. 'Reg Thorogood was in here getting his mother's shopping and he told me. It's those new people in the woods. They say they're Martin Smith the gamekeeper's parents but if you ask me, there's something fishy about them. This boy was sent to stay with them and now he's hopped it. Probably gone home, I reckon. I've heard things about the Smiths...' She tapped her broad nose with her forefinger.

'What have you heard?' Harry asked.

'My lips are sealed.' Her double chins turned to treble as she looked down at our shopping. 'Nothing for you children to bother your heads about.'

'We're teenagers, not children, Mrs Button,' Harry said crossly.

Mrs Button just laughed, her chins wobbling like jellies.

Harry frowned as she paid for the loaf of bread, the

bottle of lemonade, a bag of broken biscuits and an expensive tin of Spam because that wasn't rationed. I bought a tin of pilchards in case we found Thomasina.

The other shop in the village was a butcher called Mr Blood. The words were above the shop: *Arthur Blood: High Class Butcher*. I was still giggling about this when Harry strode ahead of me. Mr Blood was carefully wrapping up a small lamb chop in a piece of newspaper. 'Your mother's had her meat allowance this week,' he said to Harry in a gloomy voice. He was completely bald with a small black moustache, rather like Hitler's.

'I wondered if you had some lights,' she said. 'Or offal.'

It didn't seem to be the right shop to buy lights of any sort and I had no idea what offal was.

'Got another dog, then?' He was burrowing under the counter. 'I was sorry to hear of the accident. Nearly got run over myself by an Army motorcycle. They go much too fast through Hogsty End. There will be more deaths, I'm sure. But what can you expect, in wartime? And now there's this missing lad. Most likely Martin's parents at Keeper's Cottage didn't treat him right. Martin's a funny one, when he's here. Never goes to the Sow and Pigs. Just stays in the woods. Keeps himself to himself. There's something funny about him. Some say he's a foreigner.'

The 'lights' weren't electric light bulbs but revolting pinky-white lumps that Harry said were cow's lungs and the offal turned out to be greyish liver. As he wrapped them, he droned on, nodding at me, 'My brother Clem's going to do some work on your house soon as he can. Rushed off his feet, with his son in the Army.'

When we were walking back, I said, 'They're pretty nosy in this village, aren't they? It isn't like that in London.'

'I've heard you could drop down dead in London and nobody would care,' Harry said.

Before I could think of a reply, there was a splutter of exhausts as a file of Army motorcyclists came zooming past. 'Far too fast,' Harry said. 'I came back from school one day and found a motorcyclist had had an accident on our corner – before you turn up our track. Mum was covering the soldier with a horse-blanket and she wouldn't let me look but sent me to ring for an ambulance. She told me afterwards that he was dead – cracked his head open like an egg.'

I felt a bit sick and the ground seemed to move under my feet. Before the war, I only thought of old people dying but now, death was everywhere.

'Better leave Max's food hidden under your bed,' Harry said as we trudged up the rutty track to the farm.

Then we saw a bike propped up against the yard gate. 'I wonder who that is?' she said.

We soon found out as we took Mrs Seddon's bit of shopping into the kitchen. PC Thorogood was sitting at the table, biting into a piece of cake. 'Oh, there you are, Pippa,' Mum said. 'Some poor boy has run away.'

'Seen anyone, Harry?' Mrs Seddon asked. 'We never get out of here except for haymaking and the market, do we, Dick?' She looked at her husband who didn't answer but went on stirring his tea, round and round.

'Very good cake,' said the policeman, slurping his tea.

'It's war-cake. No fat, one egg, flour, and lots of currants left over from better days. And mixed with left-over tea,' she said. I wondered if she meant the dregs from our cups.

''Course, you got your own eggs.' PC Thorogood looked pointedly at the bowl of eggs on the dresser.

'Just enough for us and a few friends,' Mrs Seddon said quickly. 'About this boy?'

'Well, by all accounts that old couple aren't the best folk to look after an evacuee,' the policeman said. 'The old man shouldn't be allowed to use Martin's gun, for a start, but it's not illegal. And Mrs Smith's not well. Told me she was run off her feet, coping. She's worried about Martin, too. There's been no news of him since Dunkirk.'

Dick Seddon looked up then. 'The stupid bloody government's trying to make out it wasn't just a bloody shambles. They make out it was a triumph, saving thousands of men. But we lost thousands, too, dead or in prison. To say nothing of those poor bloody French refugees the Jerries machine-gunned to bits.'

PC Thorogood looked uncomfortable and mopped the sweat off his brow. The stove and the sun coming through the window made the kitchen very hot. He lumbered to his feet. 'I'd best be going,' he said. 'The boy's nearly twelve and he's got very fair hair – almost white. Small for his age. If you children see anything of the lad, try to talk to him, bring him back. Ten to one he'll be home any time now, starving hungry.'

'I expect so,' I said, crossing my fingers behind my back. 'I suppose you've not seen our cat, Thomasina? She's black with a white front and four white paws.'

He said he hadn't, sorry, and lumbered out.

I thought looking for Thomasina would be a good excuse to get back to the den and feed poor Max. I looked at Mum, who had been sitting quietly all this time, I thought probably rather shocked by Dick Seddon's swearing. 'Harry said she'd help me have another look for Thomasina in the woods,' I said.

'She's very probably gone back to the cottage,' Mum said. 'I'm walking up to the forces' canteen with someone the Vicar knows, to help for a few hours today and I'll try to look in on the way back. She won't have gone far.'

'Unless she's been eaten by a fox.' Or shot by a mad old man, I thought.

There was a wild honking from the geese and a knock on the door and a uniformed postman walked in, panting. He was stooped and grey-haired. 'Morning, Percy,' said Mrs Seddon. 'Tea?'

To my surprise, Dick Seddon looked up and smiled. 'Morning, Sarge,' he said.

The postman drew himself up and saluted, grinning.

'Percy was in the same Regiment, but in the last war,' Mrs Seddon explained.

'Yes.' He tapped his leg. 'That's why I limp. Got wounded at Wipers.'

'A place called Ypres,' Mum said to me in her instructive voice. 'There were battles there in the last war.'

59

'That was the war to end all wars, wasn't it?' Dick Seddon said. 'Didn't work, did it? This won't be the last war, either. It's all those bloody leaders – invading other countries. Fear and greed makes the world go round.' He slumped back in his chair as if he had exhausted himself. 'But we got to defend ourselves. Mel thinks you should just let people kill you. Turn the other cheek – my foot!'

I wanted to giggle at the way he'd put it but Mrs Seddon said reprovingly, 'The Quakers are good people, Dick.'

'Religion! God's on our side and everyone else is wrong. Religious people kill the ones who don't agree with them.'

'Not the Quakers, Dad,' Harry said. 'They won't kill anyone.'

He grunted angrily.

'Dick's always been reading books,' Mrs Seddon said apologetically, as if reading was something bad.

We were all silent. I felt sorry for Mel, not here to defend herself. And I felt sorry for Dick Seddon. I could feel him bottled up with anger as if some day he might explode.

But maybe he was right about wars. Each school I went to started history lessons with the Normans invading England but those battles seemed so far off that the bloody bits didn't matter. And there were Vikings wearing horns on their helmets, invading before that. I suppose I'm descended from lots of invading foreigners.

'I'm afraid you're right, Dick,' Mum said rather sadly. 'And we British did our share of taking over other countries in the past.'

Percy handed the letters round. There was one for Mum and I recognised Dad's writing.

'Tell you later, Pip,' she said quietly, slipping the letter into the pocket of her dungarees.

'Nearly bought another bullet today,' Percy said, drinking his tea standing up. 'Martin's dad. He was waving a gun out of the window. I left the post on top of the gate while Mrs Smith called out some excuse that the fox had taken some of their chickens. She works at the Manor, cleaning for those government people. But I'm not surprised that boy's done a runner. The wife looks done in and the old man's a bag of nerves. Not right for a lad of that age.' He turned to go, then said, 'There was a letter addressed to them only the name was Schmidt. S C H M I DT,' he spelled it out. 'So they must be Germans. Changed their names to Smith. No wonder Martin never talked about them. He was probably ashamed of being German. The whole thing's a bit fishy, if you ask me.'

'So Max was telling the truth,' I said to Harry, as we went to catch the ponies afterwards.

'Seems like it,' Harry said, grabbing Silver's halter.

We'd promised Mum and Mrs Seddon that we'd only go out for an hour, to look for Thomasina and give the ponies some exercise. Market day was tomorrow and we were to help pick vegetables for the Seddons' stall.

I was pleased that Bracken came up to me as soon as

I held the apples out. Perhaps he was looking forward to nipping me again!

Harry held the ponies while I went to fetch the food. We'd stuffed it in two old haversacks that we could carry on our backs.

I found Mum sitting on her bed with an open letter beside her. The heat brought out the smell of the liver and lights and I thought she'd ask me what was in the bags. She blew her nose and looked away quickly but not before I saw she'd been crying.

I was filled with fear. 'What is it? Is Dad all right?'

'Bit of hay fever.' She wiped her eyes.

'There's something wrong.'

'No. Nothing,' she said in a muffled voice.

I don't know what made me swoop on the letter. She was strict about things like that – she'd never read my diary and I never read her letters – and she tried to snatch it back but not before I read in my father's neat writing: '*Just to say leave is cancelled at the moment . . .*' My eyes scanned the page. '*. . . hope you and Pippa are managing . . . I hate to break it to you in a letter but I have met someone else. She's an ATS girl called Netta and we are deeply in love . . .*'

At that moment, Mum snatched the letter from me. 'You've no business . . .' she began but I interrupted, 'Is it true? He loves someone else?'

'So it seems,' she said, whispering.

Then we sort of blundered into a big hug. 'I've got to go,' she said, breaking away. 'Don't worry, Pippa. It's the war – it changes people. And your father loves you.'

I was suddenly filled with anger. How could Dad

upset her like that! Mum was the best person in the world. How could he prefer this awful Netta? 'Well, I don't love him!' I shouted. 'I hope he crashes his plane and dies!' I heard Harry calling so I picked up the bags and ran out of the hut. I certainly didn't want Harry to see my poor mum in tears.

'You were ages,' Harry said.

I was so angry I couldn't answer and I just gave her one of the bags and flung myself onto Bracken, giving him a kick so he trotted over the field ahead of Harry. My thighs and back hurt with every jolt but I didn't care.

Harry mustn't see me crying.

Chapter 7

I managed to undo the wire on the gate and left it open for Harry and Silver. Bracken stood stock still as I launched myself onto his back again and very nearly fell off the other side.

'Are you trying to race me?' she called. 'Watch you don't fall off!'

By the time she caught up with me, I'd stopped crying but I was so angry with Dad that I couldn't speak. She gave me more riding instructions and I suppose I tried to listen but in my head I was writing an angry letter to Dad. When he'd left us at Rose Cottage he'd said, 'Now, Pipsqueak' – the name he'd called me when I was small – 'I know you'll look after Mummy and behave yourself,' and he'd given me a farewell hug. 'See you soon as I can,' he'd promised. The thought of it now made me feel sick.

'Are you OK?' Harry asked.

'Yes,' I muttered. I think she was going to ask me questions only Winston burst through the bushes, so suddenly that Bracken skipped sideways (Harry told me later it was called shying) and I fell off.

The path was soft but it hurt, all the same, and Winston didn't help because he was licking my face as he stood over me, obviously worried.

Harry got off and held Winston while I struggled up,

rubbing my shoulder.

'You'll have to learn to grip with your knees,' she said maddeningly. 'Wait till Mum's put a penny between your knee and the saddle. It's hard to keep it there!'

I wasn't listening properly because I thought I heard voices and faint screaming. 'Someone's found Max!' I whispered.

'Let's lead the ponies and creep up quietly – it's not far from here,' Harry said.

Winston ran ahead and then stopped, waiting for us.

Now we could hear a boy's voice shouting, 'Man the machine-gun! That Stukka's diving and it'll get us!!' He made low screaming sounds and ack-ack noises as we peered through the bushes at the side of the cave.

'Untie me!' Max was shouting from somewhere.

Two boys were kneeling, looking upwards and aiming guns at the patch of sky between the branches. 'There it goes!' yelled one and he actually fired the gun.

The noise echoed through the woods, making Bracken jerk back so I lost the reins. Winston rushed forward, into the bushes.

'It's Spike and the evacuee,' Harry said. 'Spike's shooting at a pheasant. Other boy's got a piece of wood. Catch Bracken. We'll charge them!' She got on Silver and rode straight at the boys. Bracken was too quick for me, following Silver, so I ran after them, telling myself not to be scared of the gun.

Bracken's sturdy rump ahead of me hid what was happening but I heard a yell, then Winston barking and I saw a boy was holding on to Silver's reins and

65

laughing. 'Nearly ran me down!' he said in a nasty voice. 'A good thing you fell off!'

The other boy was just standing, looking scared and a scream came from the cave. 'Pip – get Max!' Harry shouted, head-butting the boy, who reeled back, letting Silver go.

I found Max in the den, trying to hobble in a sack tied round his waist. 'It's all right,' I said. 'Keep still,' as I fumbled with the thin rope that bound his hands behind his back.

He was incoherent with tears but stammered out, 'Spike says I'm his prisoner... I'm kidnapped.'

'You bloody idiot, Spike!' Harry was yelling outside.

'I'll tell unless you pay me!' Spike yelled back and then I heard yowls and slaps as they fought. I undid Max's wrists and the sack and we ran to the opening.

The other boy stood, white-faced, holding Bracken while Harry and Spike were aiming wild blows at each other. Already Spike's nose was bleeding. 'Stop it!' I shouted. 'You can't hit a girl!'

He took no notice. Harry was dodging the next blow when Winston, carrying a dead pheasant, came charging into the battle, tripping Harry up and Spike seized his chance, pinning Harry to the ground. 'I'll tell the police you've got him unless you give me money.'

A surge of anger filled me and I hammered on his rock-hard back. 'Let her go!' I yelled and then I saw Max running into the bushes, followed by Winston.

'Benny – get after him,' Spike was shouting at the other boy.

Benny pulled himself onto Bracken and rode after Max.

Then I heard the familiar, uneven beat of Enemy airplanes approaching and the air-raid siren wailed its alarm. I was still pulling at Spike's shoulders and suddenly he fell backwards, swearing loudly and knocking me down. I could see the planes now, through a big gap in the trees overhead. They were flying low and again I saw those deadly black crosses on the wings.

Spike yelled, 'Them's German planes!' and ran off, crashing through the bushes.

Harry was scrambling up, her face bloody. We both saw Silver tossing his head, ears back, and dived for the loose reins. We just got him in time, then, 'Look!' shouted Harry and we saw one plane lay a shining egg, dropping through the sky... I just had time to think that the cave would be safe but we couldn't leave Silver, then the bomb exploded somewhere near with a terrific thud, hurting my ears and sending all the birds in the air. We hung on to Silver as he panicked, rearing in the air like a circus horse.

It was like the time after the bomb exploded by our cottage. There was a strange stillness, as if the world had stopped. Silver, sweating and tense, stood between us and I found myself automatically stroking his wet neck. The noise of the planes rumbled into the distance and we heard the long siren call of the All Clear.

'Bloody hell! That was close,' Harry said. 'I hope the farm's OK. We've got to find Bracken. Get on behind me. Which way did he go?'

'Over there – through the bushes,' I said.

Silver was smaller than Bracken and I managed to get on his slippery, sweaty back behind Harry. The pony was still shocked from the bomb and shot forward. We both had to cling on and lie low on his back. The path was merely a tiny track some animal had made and it went straight downhill so I was glad to hang on to Harry.

'That explosion would make Bracken bolt with that bloody evacuee,' Harry said. 'I bet he's fallen off and I hope he's broken his neck.'

She was so angry she seemed to have forgotten about Max. He must be terrified after his ordeal and then hearing the bomb explode.

We seemed to spend ages slithering downhill and then we heard crying. Silver stopped abruptly. Benny lay across our path, groaning and clutching his leg. We slid off the pony and Harry stood over Benny. 'Where's Bracken?' she asked angrily.

'Fell off, didn't I?' he said. 'I didn't want to tie up that boy, honest. Me leg's broken and I hurt all over.' Tears streamed down his face. 'I only rode the carthorse before. I want my mam. I want to go home!'

'Your fault stealing Bracken,' Harry said. Before I could stop her, she hoisted him under the arms. He screamed as she dragged him along.

I'd gone to some of Mum's Red Cross classes. 'You shouldn't move him,' I said.

She'd propped him against a tree-trunk at the side of the path. 'Got to get him out of the way,' she said. He swayed, grey-faced. 'Come on,' she said. 'We must find Bracken or he might get on the road.'

I was shocked. 'But Benny's hurt. We can't just leave him.'

Harry glared at me. Blood was dripping down from her cut lip and her face was dirty where Spike had pushed her down. 'He shouldn't have taken Bracken – or tied up Max,' she yelled.

'All you think about is your animals!' I shouted. 'Benny's hurt and what about Max?'

Afterwards, I thought I'd not been fair. Only a little while ago I'd been more worried about having to move Thomasina again than about England being invaded.

Now I said, 'I'm staying with Benny till you get help for him.'

'Siding with the enemy,' she hissed and got on Silver, riding off at speed.

I hated her then. I bet if she was a soldier she'd shoot all the prisoners.

'Thanks for staying,' Benny said. Then he swayed. His face was dead white. 'Feel funny,' he said, and slumped sideways onto the ground.

I could hear my heart thumping in my ears. Flies buzzed round Benny's snotty face but he didn't move. Was he dead?

Would Harry come back? If she didn't – what could I do?

Chapter 8

I tried to remember the Red Cross class. Didn't you have to look for a pulse? I took his limp wrist and couldn't feel anything. Panic rising, I tried shouting at him. 'Benny, wake up!'

After what seemed ages but probably wasn't more than a minute, he opened his eyes. 'Hurts,' he muttered. 'Thirsty.'

I realised I was still wearing my rucksack. I brought out the bottle of lemonade. At once Benny sat up, grabbed the bottle and pulled out the cork. Lemonade fizzed all over his face and mouth as he drank, adding to the mess on his face.

'We'd better get back,' I said, wondering how. 'Where does your leg hurt?'

'Low down. It's me ankle. That boot's killing me.'

I looked. He was wearing laced hobnailed boots. The flesh between the end of his trousers and the top of the boot was red and puffy. I undid the laces and pulled as gently as I could but he yelled out. 'You're killing me!'

His ankle was swollen already.

I tried to think of the Red Cross book. Mum had got me to test her so she could pass her First Aid exam. His ankle might be broken or just twisted. Bandages ... bathing with cold water. Strips of cloth – well, I wasn't going to take *my* shirt off.

'Take off your shirt,' I ordered.

His pale face flushed. 'Don't want to.'

'Don't be stupid. I'd never fancy you in a million years!'

He undid the buttons and took it off, his face scarlet now, instead of white. The shirt had a hole on the sleeve which made it easier for me to tear it up.

'Hey! I only got two shirts. Mum'll go mad if she finds out!' he said but I took no notice. I soaked the material with the remains of the lemonade and bound up his ankle. It was more of a bundle than a bandage and Benny didn't help because he said I was making the pain worse.

Harry hadn't come back. 'We'll have to walk back,' I told Benny.

I helped him up. He was about my height but heavier, I found as he leaned against me. He smelled of sweat. I didn't want him hanging on to me but there wasn't any other way. 'Put your arm round my shoulders,' I ordered.

'Good thing me mates can't see me now, leaning on a girl,' he muttered as we shuffled slowly along.

Mum always said if you got lost, don't go on, retrace your steps. I hadn't a clue where I was so I headed back, up the hill towards the den. I thought I could easily find hoof-marks from there, back to the farm.

Benny moaned a bit and then cursed Spike, using words I'd not heard before. 'Spike done a runner on me and I never wanted to hurt that boy,' he said. 'He's an evacuee same as me and wants to get home like I do.'

71

Suddenly I felt sorry for him. 'Is it horrible at the farm, then?'

''S OK – food's good – more'n we have at home – but that Spike's worse'n Hitler. He's older and stronger than me. Makes me do all the nasty work at the farm and pretends to his mam and dad he's done it. Says I'm a soft Londoner. I'd be all right without him around.'

I thought about Max. If he came back to the den, Spike might bring the policeman along.

'Promise you'll stop him telling about Max, then,' I said. 'Or we'll tell about you tying him up.'

'I'll try,' he promised. 'Where do you think that bomb landed?'

I'd been so busy I'd not thought at all. Now I had a cold feeling. Supposing it had landed on the Seddons' house? I remembered with relief that Mum was safe at the canteen. Then I felt guilty. Even if Harry had been horrible, deserting Benny and me, she didn't deserve anything happening to her parents.

It took ages to get up that hilly path to the den, where we collapsed on the ground in front. Max's sack lay at the entrance. 'What's that awful smell?' Benny asked.

Harry had left the rucksack on the ground when she fought Spike. 'The dog meat's gone rotten,' I said. Then I had an idea. 'Why don't you stay here, in the cave out of the sun, and I'll get help.'

'You might not come back,' Benny said, sitting up.

'I promise.'

He turned his head and I saw his large dark eyes were

glistening with unshed tears. He brushed his dirty hand across his eyes and frowned, obviously cross with himself. 'I don't want to stay here all alone. I never been to the country before and it's too quiet and yet there's funny noises. Spike said it was a fox crying out last night but it sounded like someone being done in.'

Spike had taken his shotgun with him but I saw Benny's stick on the ground. I knew I was soft but I couldn't help being sorry for him. 'OK. We'll go on. You lean on that stick as well as me.'

I chose the proper track that Harry and I had ridden along, that first time we came to the den. Using the stick, Benny didn't lean so heavily on me but all the same, I felt so tired and hot that I wondered if we'd make it all the way back.

Then I heard the soft clopping of hooves behind us. Harry was there, on Silver. 'You should've left him,' she said crossly. 'I couldn't find Bracken and there's no sign of Max or the dog.'

'Benny's got to see the doctor.' I glared at her. She looked a mess, with dried blood congealing from a cut on her cheek. 'You're a stinking pig, leaving me! Worse than a pig,' I added, thinking that the Seddons' pigs looked much more friendly than Harry.

She swiped a fly off her face. 'Sorry,' she mumbled, to my amazement. 'Help me haul him onto Silver. He doesn't deserve help, going off with Bracken like that. You look done in. Sit behind him.'

Benny protested weakly as we got him onto Silver's back. I'd lost any spring I'd learned and Harry had to give me a leg up. I stared at Benny's naked back, red with sunburn and running with sweat and reluctantly put my arms round his waist. Harry led us along. Every time Silver stumbled, my face went into Benny's neck and his wiry black hair tickled my nose. My sweaty hands slithered on his skin.

'Gawd! If Spike saw me he'd wet himself laughing,' Benny complained. 'Stuck to a girl, like this!'

'Shut up about Spike,' Harry snapped. 'This isn't the first fight we've had. He thinks all the girls should be after him. And do what he says. He goes on about my hair. Next time, I'll kill him!'

I wondered if this was why wars began.

Someone was calling my name. We rounded the bend and met Mrs Seddon, Mum, a youngish man in RAF uniform and a very large red-faced man. 'They're all right!' Mum shouted, running towards us.

'We heard the bomb was in the woods somewhere,' Mrs Seddon said. 'That pony looks done in, Harry. What have you been up to? And where's Bracken?'

'I had to leave off harvesting to find you, Benny,' the large man said. 'What's wrong with your leg? Spike's run off, taking my gun without asking.'

'Hey there! The kids are OK – that's the main thing, isn't it?' said the airman. He sounded American or something. 'Your mum heard the siren and the bomb dropping and I gave her a lift on my motorbike back. I just hope the journey didn't make your hay fever worse, Alice.' He smiled at Mum.

'I'm fine and very grateful to you, Don.' Mum gave a

74

tight little smile and I saw that her eyes were puffy and swollen. She didn't get hay fever. She must have been crying her eyes out on that long walk to the canteen. I hated my father even more. How could he find anyone else nicer than Mum?

Don and Mr Wilson helped Benny back to the farm. Then Mum and Don had to go, Don back on duty at the RAF station nearby and Mum to the canteen. Mum made me promise to be sensible 'for a change, Pip. I am relying on you'.

The nearest doctor was in Felford eight miles away, so Harry tracked down Nurse Robin, who pronounced that Benny's ankle was twisted, not broken. She also washed and put a plaster on Harry's cheek.

All the time Mrs Seddon went on at us about losing Bracken and getting into a fight. 'So irresponsible, Harry,' she said.

'Bloody selfish to worry everyone,' Dick Seddon muttered. 'We thought the bomb had landed on you.'

'It wasn't her fault,' Benny said unexpectedly.

Harry looked at him and for a moment I thought she was going to say what really happened but she didn't speak.

'I'm going to get to the bottom of this when that boy of mine comes back,' Mr Wilson said in a threatening voice and he took Benny off in an ancient truck, muttering about all the harvesting time he was losing to say nothing of his petrol.

Nurse Robin came into the kitchen for a cup of tea. 'I heard from Bob Thorogood that the bomb fell in the

Manor grounds,' she said. 'Maybe the Germans had found out about those Government people at the Manor House.' She tapped her nose. 'Some say they're not just from Government offices but they're being trained for special duties.'

She stopped to sip her tea and I butted in. 'Aren't we supposed to *Keep Mum* and what about *Tittle Tattle Lost the Battle*?'

Nurse Robin frowned at me. 'There used to be a saying that "children should be seen and not heard",' she snapped. 'Mrs Jarvis thinks we may have spies living amongst us, sending off radio messages to the Enemy. Those Smiths in the wood are Germans, they say. But I'm telling you just between these four walls.'

'*Walls have Ears*,' I said, quoting the poster and she glared at me. Dick Seddon got up, pushing his chair back so abruptly that it fell over. 'They ought to put the lot of them in prison till this bloody war's finished.' And he went out.

Nurse Robin smiled triumphantly. 'That's what I said to Mrs Jarvis,' and she went to fetch her bicycle.

After we'd rubbed down Silver and let her loose, we had a very late lunch and Harry got told off for fighting. 'Girls shouldn't fight,' said her father.

Harry looked up, an angry glint in her eyes. 'I thought you believed in defending yourself. I didn't know you were a pacifist like Mel, Dad.'

Of course he told her to leave the table and I followed. 'And you can look for that pony,' he shouted after her. 'On your feet. That'll teach you.'

'And come back in an hour,' Mrs Seddon said. 'I'm going down the village to tell people to look out for Bracken. Supposing he's on the roads?'

I was so hot and tired I couldn't eat, anyway. I kept worrying about Max. Had he run off home after all?

'Telling me not to fight. He hasn't a clue,' Harry muttered as we walked up the field, carrying the bucket filled with chopped up apples and bread crusts. It was hotter than ever and Auntie was snoozing in the shade of a bush, in no mood to rush at anyone.

'We've got to find Max,' I said as soon as we were in the wood.

'I don't know why we're bothering. He's probably miles away by now,' Harry said. 'Did you hear Nurse Robinson? The village thinks the Smiths are spies. If we find him, he'll get sent back to them but he could find proof they're spies and tell us. Dad might be proud of me if I helped catch enemy spies. After all, the next bomb might be right on top of the Manor House.'

'But Mrs Smith works there. She wouldn't want to be bombed.'

'She'd tell them – in code, of course – what time to come.'

Was Harry right? If we ever found Max we could ask if the Smiths had a special wireless transmitter – I'd no idea what it would be like but I'd heard of them.

We went on banging that bucket through the woods but only scared the birds. Harry kept looking for hoof-marks but found only the ones we'd originally made;

they petered out where the hot sun had shafted through the trees and dried the earth.

We'd gone along a new path and I noticed the woods thinning out and a field ahead.

'Where are we?' I asked.

'Must be near the back of your old home. We'd better get back or we'll be in more trouble.' Harry turned and began walking away.

I thought about poor Thomasina, now almost forgotten in the search for Max and Bracken. 'I just want to see if our cat has gone home,' I called. 'We can have a drink – and I think there's some of Mum's home-made biscuits in the tin.'

She followed me reluctantly over a stile and across the dried-up grass. So much had happened that it already seemed ages since we'd crept up the edge of the same field to rescue Thomasina.

The sun had disappeared behind yellow-grey clouds but it was still very hot. I thought longingly of sitting in the cool cottage, drinking Mum's home-made lemonade which must still be on the stone shelf in the larder, covered with a little net against flies.

We walked down the garden and the front of the cottage gaped at us. Someone had put a notice outside, written in chalk on a board, *Danger*. Harry looked at it. 'Do you think it will all come tumbling down?' she asked. 'I'm scared of being buried alive ever since I was little and tried to go down a hole to find a rabbit like Alice in Wonderland. It all fell in on top of me and it was horrible.'

I couldn't believe this was Harry talking. 'Mum's been inside,' I said but my heart beat fast as I trod over rubble and our sad-looking broken furniture. I thought I heard something shift but it was in the kitchen. That door was still intact.

Thirst drove me on. I opened the door and Winston rushed at me, nearly knocking me over. There was a hiss from the top of the dresser where Thomasina was puffed out with hate.

'If Winston's shut in here that means...'

Harry didn't finish as I opened the larder door and saw the dim shape of a boy, crouched under the shelf.

Chapter 9

'No – I won't go back!' Max whimpered, still curled up like a baby, his thumb in his mouth.

Winston went to stand in front of him, wagging his tail and growling at us as if he didn't know which to do.

'You can't stay here,' I said. 'There's going to be someone coming to mend the cottage and my mum's looking in, too.'

Harry pushed past me, patted Winston and ordered him to come back and sit. To my surprise he did. Then she crouched down to speak to Max. 'We've got a special mission for you. Very important,' she said.

'Those horrible boys will come and get me,' Max whispered. 'I hid because I thought you were them.'

'No – they won't. I've just bashed one of them on the nose and the other's hurt his ankle. Come on out, Max. We've got this plan for you and then you can be a hero, catching spies.'

'I want to go home,' Max muttered but he came out, covered in cobwebs and dirt. His face was scratched and his eyelids were swollen.

'Have you eaten anything?' I asked him.

'Biscuits,' he said. 'And lemonade from a jug. And I opened a can of sardines for Winston. The cat wouldn't come down.'

At least he hadn't been too scared to do that. Harry dusted him down with hard pats, as if he were a pony. 'You'll have to be brave,' she said. 'You know you can't go back to your old home. But what we want you to do is to find evidence that the Smiths are spies. Then we can get them arrested and you can...' She paused because obviously neither of us could think what would happen to poor Max.

He wasn't listening, anyway, but fidgeting from one foot to another. 'I wanna go,' he said desperately. 'I didn't dare go in the garden in case those boys came.'

I felt very sorry for him. 'I'll take you,' I said. What he needed was a bath and a good meal.

'Don't let him out of your sight. We haven't briefed him yet,' Harry said.

I thought 'briefing' sounded very efficient. I wondered if she'd heard the word on the wireless.

Max rushed into the outside lavatory and I waited with Winston, who sat, guarding the door. Suddenly he growled.

Spike came charging through the kitchen garden, still carrying the gun. I felt ashamed afterwards but I couldn't help screaming. He looked awful, with blood streaked down his face and oozing from his nose. 'Where's that boy?' he shouted, waving the gun. I hoped it wasn't still loaded.

Winston, tail wagging and growling in his usual confused way, was jumping up at Spike, stopping him. Harry must have heard me scream because she came out of the cottage and shouted, 'I hate you! And your dad's looking for you. He's hopping mad!'

81

'You've done my nose in,' Spike yelled at Harry. 'Call yourself a sodding girl! I'll get you and I'll get that German boy.'

'We've not seen him!' I said.

'Liar!' Spike rushed past us to the cottage.

'Come out quickly, Max,' Harry whispered at the lavatory door. 'He's gone into the house.'

There was a strange swooshing sound and a yell from the cottage. I looked round and saw a cloud of dust coming out of a jagged hole in the roof. Then Thomasina rushed out, a ghost cat covered in plaster. I ran towards her but she shot into the bushes. At least she was all right and I guessed she'd stay in the garden when we'd gone.

Winston barked excitedly, Harry laughed and shouted to Max, 'The roof's fallen in on Spike!'

Max came out and Harry dragged him by the arm, up the track. 'Come on, hurry!' she shouted impatiently at me.

'But Spike might be hurt,' I said.

'Serves him right.'

I ran after them. I thought I heard a faint cry of 'help' from the cottage. Supposing Spike was badly injured?

Max stumbled along, obviously tired out. Harry held one arm and I held the other.

'See – the police will find you anyway but you'll be in less trouble if you go back to Keeper's Cottage yourself,' Harry was saying. 'All you've got to do is to find out about the Smiths spying and then we can get them taken away.'

'Max – have they got one of those wireless transmitter things – to send out messages or Morse code?' I asked.

His answer was so faint that I had to bend down to hear it. 'There's something in a locked room in the attic. I'm not allowed up there but *he* goes there and shoots at the foxes and rats from the window.'

'That'll be where it is,' Harry said triumphantly. 'Try to get in there and hide. And then you can look in Mrs Smith's pockets when she comes back from the Manor. She probably steals secret documents when she's cleaning.'

'But how shall I find you to tell?' Max asked in a miserable voice.

'We'll watch the house from the bushes just above. When could you get out?'

'Don't know. They'll watch me all the time now.' He slowed down, dragging his feet and I knew he was scared of going back.

'You'll have to come after dark when they're asleep. They're old so they won't stay up late.'

'He's got that gun.'

'You've got to be brave, like the soldiers are,' Harry said.

I remembered what Mum had said and added a bit. 'You don't want them to signal to the Germans to bomb the village, do you? Or to send soldiers by parachute so the Nazis capture the whole of England?'

He broke loose from us both. 'No!' he shouted. 'I hate the bloody Germans for killing my mum!' I noticed that he admitted now she was dead. 'But promise you'll tell the police as soon as I've got proof?'

'I promise – cross my throat and hope to die if I break

it,' Harry said, her forefinger slicing across her neck. 'We'll come back tomorrow night about eleven and show a little light from a torch. You can signal back. No plane's going to see that light through the woods.' Typical Harry, she'd not thought that it would be almost as difficult for us to get away as it would be for Max.

The heat was oppressive now and thunder rumbled above the treetops. The wood was silent and growing darker, almost like evening.

Harry looked up apprehensively. 'Going to be a storm,' she said. 'I hate thunder and lightning.'

I was surprised again at Harry being scared. Mum and I used to enjoy looking out of the window of our top-floor flat in Eastbourne at the storm lashing the sea, lightning flashing over the white-topped waves.

We were now at the beginning of the path which divided, one way to Keeper's Cottage and the other up the hill, towards home. Sheets and towels still flapped, pale in the gloom but there was no other movement. Winston started forward towards his old home, then sat down as if he were awaiting orders.

'I can't go back!' Max said again. 'He'll beat me!'

Suddenly I felt really sorry for him and wanted to help. 'I'll take you. I'll tell them I found you lost in the woods,' I said. 'And I promise we'll come back.'

'Let him go on his own,' Harry began and then we heard a faint whinnying from further up the path. Harry rushed off and called back, 'It's Bracken! His reins are caught up by a branch.'

'Come on,' I said and I took Max's hand and marched

him up the track to the cottage, Winston beside us.

My heart hammered in my ribs as I wondered if the mad German would leap out with his gun and shoot us both!

Chapter 10

I knocked on the door. Nothing happened. I heard Winston panting beside me and a distant sound of thunder. 'Maybe they've died,' Max said hopefully but there were sounds of unbolting and the door opened a crack, held back by a chain. A pale old face peeped through. '*Mein Gott!* Maximillian!' the old woman said.

'I found him in the woods, lost,' I said very quickly as the door opened. So he was really called Maximillian – what a dreadful name to have at school!

To my surprise Mrs Smith rushed at Max and hugged him tightly. 'Oh, I thought you were gone like your poor dear Mutti and then there was the bomb, driving my poor husband mad – and nobody to ask where it landed.' She had a foreign accent, too, so everyone was right about the Smiths being Germans.

'In the grounds of the Manor House,' I said quickly, to test her reactions.

Her head jerked up. 'Are they all right there?'

She obviously felt guilty about the bomb. 'I don't know. Probably,' I said.

Max suddenly clung to her long, old-fashioned black skirts. 'Don't let him beat me!'

'My Hans never would. It's all talk and he is a sick

86

man,' she said to me, pulling at a wisp of her grey hair that had escaped from her bun. Then she lowered her voice. 'He's asleep now but we must be quiet. He was in the British Army in the First World War – you know about that, *liebchen*?'

'Sort of,' I said, vaguely remembering a lesson at school.

'Very terrible. His friend's head was blown off, in the trench beside him. He got ill – gas got his lungs and then he had shell shock. It's like having very bad nerves. They gave him electric shocks but it made him worse. And now with this new war he's got very bad.' She felt in the big pocket of her apron and brought out a handkerchief. Was she acting a part or...?

I hadn't got time to decide. There was a wheezy shout from an upstairs window and I looked up from the doorstep. This time, a flash of lightning showed me the glint of metal. He was pointing the gun down at me!

Max had seen it too. 'Hide me!' he cried out, and Mrs Smith swept him inside saying to me, 'Run, run fast!'

I did and heard the huge bang as the gun fired and the loud cries of the crows, alarmed out of the trees.

Nothing seemed to have hit me so I ran until I was hidden by the bushes on the path. Then I looked through a gap. Winston was pawing at the closed front door and something was going on at that upstairs window, movements and shouting. The glint of metal had gone.

Thunder rolled and rain sheeted down through the trees. Much further up the path I found Harry, with her face pressed into Bracken's side. Could she be scared?

'Didn't you hear the gun go off?' I asked, angry with her for leaving me.

'No!' she said in a muffled voice. 'What happened?'

I told her, shouting against the storm. 'Perhaps she made that up about the last war,' Harry said. 'He wouldn't have fought against his own country. We'd better get back before we're struck by lightning.' I was so tired and Bracken so slippery with rain that she gave me a leg up, putting me in front and then clutching at me every time lightning struck. The sturdy pony plodded up the hill, not really scared by the storm but putting his ears back when the thunder rolled.

'We might get struck by lightning under these trees,' Harry said.

She was scared! 'It doesn't happen often,' I said to cheer her up.

I was still thinking about Mrs Smith. She'd looked so tired, so worried that I began to feel she was genuine. 'I think I believe the old woman,' I said, when there was a gap in the thunder. 'I don't think they're spies.'

'Can't talk now,' Harry said in a tight voice.

Later, when we were back at home, I tried again. 'Mrs Smith's having an awful time with her husband. He's sick from the Great War whatever side he was on. I don't think she's got time to be a spy.'

'We'll see what Max finds out,' Harry said.

I knew she was reluctant to let the idea go as she wanted to show her father she could be clever and brave. I just had a feeling that something awful might happen to the Smiths and it might be our fault.

*

That night, while Mum was sitting at Mel's wooden table in the corner of our hut, writing to Dad, I lay on the lumpy camp bed and wrote in my diary: *I feel achey all over but at least we got Bracken back. Mrs Seddon asked if I'd like to share Harry's bathwater (but not the bath!) but when I saw the tin bath in the kitchen I said no even though Harry said her father would never come in. Harry was scared of the storm! We'd decided to tell her parents we'd found Max in the woods and taken him back – Harry said it was double-bluff but I wasn't sure what she meant. They've got a telephone at the farm and Harry's mum rang the police station to say what had happened. She said afterwards she was glad the poor boy had been found though it didn't sound as if he was happy with the Smiths and Mr Seddon said of course not, if they were Germans they probably treated him badly and the village should do something about it.*

I helped Harry shut up the hens and geese and she watched while I cleaned out the mouse house. Josephine Pie walked up her arm and I would have shown her the mice walking on the tightrope only Mum arrived for supper very wet and again on Don's motorbike. He says he's off-duty and he seemed to have cheered her up a bit and took her down to the Sow and Pigs for a drink. He even persuaded Mr Seddon to go with them and put him on the back of the motorbike (Mr Seddon held on with his good arm). Mum followed on Mrs Seddon's bike but she had to pedal hard!! We listened to the News while helping

Mrs Seddon pack the potatoes, carrots, etc. ready for the market. The only bit I remember was Mr Churchill saying something about we were winning the battle of Britain but we should expect big cities to be bombed. Lots of people said the war would be over by Christmas but it doesn't sound like that. I kept worrying about Spike in case he was really hurt but Harry said serves him right.

We were just going to bed when Mum and the others came back from the pub. Mum had met Clem, the butcher's brother, who said he'd been round to the cottage to see what had to be done to rebuild it and found Spike under a pile of plaster. He couldn't get him to say what had happened but took him back to the Wilsons' farm.

Don had to rush back to his RAF station or he'd be in big trouble, he said. I said it sounded like school and he said being in the RAF was, sometimes. He's Canadian and always wanted to join the Royal Air Force. He's got a freckled face and gingery hair and he sort of makes you feel cheerful when he comes in and even Mr Seddon looked a bit better. On my way out to the shed, I overheard him saying to his wife that folk were suspicious of the Smiths and thought the police ought to take them away.

I went to sleep worrying about Max. Where would he go then?

Chapter 11

The next day, I was woken early by Harry prodding me. She dumped a mug of tea by the bed. 'We've got to help get ready for the market, Dad says,' she whispered because Mum was still asleep. I'd woken in the night and seen the thin thread of Mum's torch. She was hunched up in bed, reading a letter, either Dad's letter or perhaps hers back to him, I didn't know which.

I wished I could tell him how much he was hurting her and I hoped a bomb would fall on him and the horrible Netta and blow them to bits.

'I wanted to try and catch Thomasina,' I said when we were outside. The wet grass glittered under the rising sun and the sky was stippled with fleecy little gold clouds as if the storm had never happened.

'This is more important. We need the money,' Harry said. 'Mum can't do it all by herself. Dad tried last week with his good hand but he had a dizzy spell and fell over. I reckon they sent him out of hospital too early.'

The cabbages were soaked from last night and it was hard work, cutting through their tough stems. Mrs Seddon was packing them into wooden boxes. 'Everything's so wet. It's a good thing I picked the beans and lettuces and dug the potatoes before the storm,' she said.

There was a loud squealing. I straightened my back

and saw Mr Wilson and Spike, wrestling with two young pigs. Spike didn't look our way but I could see he was rough on the pig he was handling, holding it by its hind legs and making it walk on its front legs like a wheelbarrow race, towards Mr Wilson's truck which was parked inside the field. I was pleased to see Spike had a plaster across the bridge of his nose.

Mr Seddon came through the gate and shouted something to him and Spike heaved the pig, still squealing, into the back of the truck.

'Tom Wilson's kindly helping me take those pigs to market,' Mrs Seddon said. 'I couldn't manage on my own.'

The other pig was squealing too, rough-handled by Mr Wilson. 'They're hurting the pigs,' I said.

'It's worse in the market,' said Harry. 'And they keep prodding and slapping at the cattle to make them move round the ring. Some people think animals don't matter.'

I was surprised again. I'd have thought that Harry was used to farming ways. I made another vow not to eat pig, not even my favourite, the rare sausages that the butcher allowed us.

While the Wilsons were doing up the back of the truck, the passenger door opened and Benny got out. His ankle was bandaged but he managed to hobble a little way, using a stick, and beckoned to me.

Mrs Seddon was piling boxes onto a big trolley so she didn't notice as I went to talk to Benny but Harry did. 'You can't talk to him – he's one of the Enemy!' she whispered but I took no notice.

'Spike's in big trouble for borrowing his dad's gun and going into your mum's cottage,' Benny said. 'But we heard from Reg Thorogood – who came along to give Spike a lecture – that you took that boy back to them Germans in the woods. There's trouble brewing – I heard Mr Wilson going on that it was about time the village got together to chase those Nazis out. Better tell the boy … ' He looked round. The truck was revving up noisily, giving out clouds of black exhaust and Mr Wilson was waving from the driving seat. 'Gotta go.'

I whispered to Harry what Benny had said.

'Wasn't that what we wanted?' she replied. 'Wait till we get the proof.'

We went inside for breakfast. Mum was up, cooking scrambled eggs on the old stove. 'It's so wonderful having really fresh eggs,' she said in a falsely bright voice but her eyelids were almost as red and puffy as Max's and she looked really tired.

Mum said she was going up to the canteen again. I watched her go and saw she was carrying her letter to the postbox. What had she said to Dad? I hoped she'd been really angry with him and told him what a good time she was having, seeing Don. Except she wasn't really having a good time because she was so upset.

The Seddons went off to market in their rusty little truck – Mrs Seddon said they were allowed extra petrol for this because they were farmers. I'd heard Dick Seddon insisting on going too. 'Even if I am useless,' he'd muttered angrily. 'At least I can man the stall.' We were to look after the farm and do the usual chores.

93

I kept thinking of Mum. She was being a heroine even if she wasn't being bombed, working at the canteen when she'd had such bad news. As Harry and I slopped pigswill into the troughs I was horrified to see my tears dripping into the bucket.

'What's up?' Harry asked.

'My dad's fallen for someone else and I hate him.'

'Maybe it's because of the war,' Harry said slowly. That was Mum's excuse but I remembered the time the blackout fell down and the other times I'd tried to forget.

'They've quarrelled before.'

'Everyone quarrels sometimes,' she said. 'Maybe it won't last and he'll leave his girlfriend.'

'I don't want him back!' I shouted, so loudly that one of the pigs looked up, surprised, swill dripping from its nose. 'I hate him and I hope his plane crashes so I never see him again!'

Harry touched my arm with a grimy hand. 'Come on. We've finished here. Let's go and look for your cat. We'll fetch some milk to tempt her out.'

We were in the kitchen when the postman put his head round the door. 'Letters for you. Looks like bills,' he said cheerfully. 'Any tea going?'

Harry filled a tin mug with tea and a precious spoonful of sugar and the postman drank it, propped in the doorway. 'I hear you girls found that boy and took him back to those Smiths,' he said. 'I bumped into Reg Thorogood and he'd been over there again. The old man was in bed so Reg told his wife to hide the gun from him. Reg said the boy was fetching water from the well but he ran into

94

the house looking scared. Reg asked her point-blank if they were Germans, by the way. She sort of nodded, then said they'd taken British nationality a long time ago. And she said they'd not heard from the boy's father for weeks. She doesn't know if he's dead or alive. I think she's lying about being British. I told Reg he ought to tell the Local Defence boys about the Smiths and get rid of them.'

'Do you mean shoot them as traitors?' Harry asked in a scared voice.

'No – they'll go off to an Internment Camp, I think they're called, with other fishy foreigners, till the end of the war. After all, why did that bomb land so near the Manor? And Mrs Smith works there as a cleaner ... There's no smoke without fire, mark my words!'

'So what would happen to M ... to the boy?' I asked.

'If there's no other relations, I suppose he'd have to be billeted somewhere till his dad comes home, if he has a dad. Thanks for the tea, girls.' And he pedalled off.

I knew Harry was thinking the same as me, that it would be awful to be Max.

This time, we walked down the long track from the farm to where it joined the village road. I saw the turning leading to Boar's Hill and I wondered how Mum was getting on. Was she speaking French to the Canadians – I noticed Don didn't sound at all French – or was she crying into mounds of washing-up?

We heard the rumble of Army lorries and flattened ourselves against the hedge as they lumbered by. Soldiers, sitting at the back, waved to us and one of them whistled. 'Hi, Blondie!' he shouted.

I felt my face go red. 'It's your hair,' Harry said, frowning. 'You should plait it again. You look older with it all over your shoulders.' It was sticking together with dirt last night so I'd washed it as best I could with a jug of hot water and a lump of strong-smelling soap.

Someone had already filled in the bomb crater outside Nurse Robinson's and brought out a pile of rubbish from her cottage.

At Rose Cottage, an oldish man wearing overalls was bringing out a load of plaster, tiles and broken furniture on a wheelbarrow. 'Your cottage?' he said. 'I'm Clem Blood and I'm going to rebuild Miss Robinson's cottage and yours. It'll take time.' He was panting already and I thought it certainly would take time if he was the only builder.

'My son's in the Army,' he said. 'Or he'd be helping me. Is that your cat?'

Thomasina was perched on the roof again, looking down at us and lashing her tail nervously.

I called her and Harry filled a tin bowl with the milk she'd carried but Thomasina didn't move. 'Lend you my ladder?' Clem asked. 'I think the gutter's OK to lean it on.'

The ladder was wooden and looked a bit ancient but I climbed up and Clem held it. Thomasina stood up, arching her back, mewing gently and walked up to me. I put out a hand but she skipped lightly away and leaped onto the lower roof of the outside lavatory.

She must have loosened a tile from our roof and I got down just in time to avoid a small cascade.

In the end, we gave up and left her the milk and I

dashed inside to fetch a tin of her favourite pilchards, which we opened and left by the back door.

Clem told me off. 'I've only propped up the roof in one place yet. It's not safe in there. I've already rescued that Spike. I don't know what he was up to. So you two took the lost boy back to those Germans at Keeper's Cottage, didn't you? Brave of you to face that mad old man and his gun. They say they're the gamekeeper's parents but who's to know? He never talked about them.'

He took off his cap and wiped his bald head with a large handkerchief. 'Pity the boy went back. He's not safe there with those foreigners.'

'What do you mean?' Harry asked.

'We don't want foreigners here, telling them German parachutists where to land, do we?' And he went back to work.

We didn't know what to believe. Harry said it was no good puzzling about it until we'd talked to Max and found out if he had any evidence about the Smiths being spies.

I was so tired with the heat and the early work in the garden that I fell asleep over my bread and cheese in the kitchen, my head on the table. I was woken up by the Seddons returning from market, pleased because they'd sold everything.

'Even the pigs,' I said sadly.

Dick Seddon smiled for once. 'Make a nice bit of bacon and ham,' he teased. Then he winced with pain and Mrs Seddon fetched some pills for him.

'It feels like I've still got a hand and it hurts like hell!' he said. 'Sorry, you two. I'm not much of a hero, am I?' and he went to lie down.

We did more chores, including a very smelly time cleaning out the pigsties. Big Bertha, stuffed with the unborn piglets, was left alone to lie on her side, panting.

Before we came to Hogsty End I'd imagined it would be fun to work on a farm, playing with the lambs, collecting nice clean brown eggs and picking fruit straight off the trees. Now I was beginning to realise that it was really hard mucky work, even though Mum said the Seddons' was a smallholding, not really a farm.

Mum came back for supper – or high tea, as Mrs Seddon called it. I'd hoped Don would bring her back but she said he was on duty at the RAF station this weekend.

She said she'd been to Rose Cottage on the way to fetch a case of clothes as Clem Blood had put an extra prop under the roof. She'd heard from him that we'd been there, trying to catch Thomasina. She'd also heard about Mr Smith's gun and said she was glad she didn't know before what we might have faced.

'It might be better to leave the cat there,' said Mrs Seddon. 'Cats like places more than people.'

'And your cats chase her away,' I said.

Mrs Seddon laughed. 'Well, she's a foreigner, isn't she!'

Mum looked very tired and said she was going to bed early but she insisted on helping wash the dishes.

When we'd put Auntie to bed I saw Mum sitting on the wooden step of our hut, smoking a cigarette and staring into space. 'I thought you'd given up,' I said.

'Just felt like one,' she muttered and smiled vaguely at Harry who said she'd got to check the ponies. I expect she was being tactful.

I sat beside her on the step. I'd noticed in the country that just before sunset there was a sort of special silence as the land settled into sleep. The chickens clucked sleepily from their hut and one of the pigs grunted. Somewhere far away, a dog howled and I thought of Winston, who must be missing his master, the gamekeeper.

I could just see the outline of the farm cats, crouched on the barn roof, enjoying the last rays of the sun. I'd overcome my fear of the geese and we'd driven them into their shed for the night in case the fox came, although I'd have thought they were a match for any fox.

'It's lovely in the evening,' Mum said but there was a break in her voice.

I was going to say, 'Forget Dad – he's not worth it,' but I suddenly thought that perhaps she still loved him. I didn't know what it was like to love a man but I imagined how I'd feel if Mum went off and left me behind. 'Maybe he'll get tired of her,' I said though I knew *I* wouldn't want him back now.

'There were good times in the past, Pipkin. He was so good-looking. I suppose I was swept off my feet, as they say.' She inhaled the smoke and then coughed. 'I was only nineteen – only six years older than you are now.'

'I'm never going to marry!'

'Of course you will. Not everyone is unhappy and just think, if I'd not married your father I wouldn't have you, Pip darling.'

It gave me a funny feeling to think I might never have been born.

'He wants a divorce,' she said, stubbing out the cigarette into the dust.

I didn't know anyone whose parents had divorced but I dimly remembered the last King of England, Edward, had married a divorced woman but he'd had to give his Crown to his brother, as a punishment. And lots of film stars had marriages 'dissolved' like aspirins. It sounded less painful than 'divorce'.

'We'll be all right on our own,' I said. Then I thought of friendly, freckled Don. He might be good for Mum. 'Or you could marry again – all the film stars do.' I gave her a hug and felt how thin and small she was. That made me nervous and I had the feeling I'd almost lost here at the farm, that nothing in the world was certain, that we walked on a thin crust pretending everything was fine but the ground could give way at any time and we'd go into a dark pit.

This made me think of Max's mother and gran, suddenly being blown to bits.

I tried not to cry. I had to look after Mum, now.

Chapter 12

Harry arranged to meet me outside the shed at ten-thirty.
The Seddons had been up since six so they'd go to bed
early. I wasn't so sure I'd be able to escape so easily
because I thought Mum would toss and turn, worrying.
She did, at first, but I suppose she was worn out too.
After a while, I could hear her regular breathing.

I was tired too so I had to try every possible way to
keep awake. I'd found one of Mel's old books, *Little
Women*, written ages ago, about an American family
whose father had gone to another war. I wished Dad was
like the good father in that book.

I read it and then kept looking at my watch by the thin
light of my torch. At last it was just before ten-thirty.

As I dressed, I thought if Mum woke, I'd say
something about going to the lavatory.

The moon was just rising so it wasn't pitch black
outside but I saw the black shapes of bats flitting above
me. I could just hear their high squeaks and hoped they
wouldn't land on me by mistake! Mum said the squeaks
sort of bounced off things and helped them 'see' the
way; I wondered if it was rather like the newly
discovered 'radar' Dad had told us about which would
help find enemy airplanes.

Harry came with Bracken. 'I thought it would be

quicker,' she said. 'Mum sleeps like the dead and Dad's taken his pills so he won't wake up for ages.'

She gave me a hand and I got up behind her. I nearly fell off again near the rows of vegetables, because Bracken shied at white strips of rag tied over a newly-sown bed to keep the birds away.

It was spooky and dark in the wood, with occasional pools of moonlight coming through the branches. A creature made a kind of loud bark, echoed by another and I imagined the woods full of wild dogs. 'What's that?' My voice shook a little.

'Only deer calling.'

We got off when the path sloped downhill, so Harry could guide Bracken down safely.

The moonlight glinted off the tiles on Keeper's Cottage and gleamed on a sheet left out to dry. Otherwise the house was in darkness. We shone the weak light of the torch through the gap in the bushes as a signal for Max.

All I could hear was Bracken's snuffling and scrunching as he ate leaves off a tree. We waited for ages and Harry was just saying, 'I bet he's spilled the beans and told them. He's probably in it too. Let's go back,' when there was a glow-worm gleam below, by the side of the house.

'That's Max!' I whispered, although nobody could hear us so far away.

The faint light danced towards us uncertainly. 'Better go and meet him,' I said, sorry for poor little Max in the dark.

Harry tied Bracken up and we stumbled down the slope.

The moon came out from behind a cloud. Max, white-faced, was only wearing pyjamas and his feet were bare. 'I can't stay,' he said, panting. 'They may have heard me. The back door bolt makes a noise.'

'So what have you found out?' Harry asked.

'Nothing. Mr Smith's lungs are bad and he's in bed. I found the key in his jacket and went up to the attic while Mrs Smith was in the kitchen.'

'What did you find?' Harry asked.

'A chair and table, his gun, lots of books, photo albums and pictures on the wall of mountains and little villages and men in funny hats and little shorts and brownish photos of soldiers sitting in rows, stamp albums, bird books, binocs. I thought I found a strange machine but it was an old gramophone, the sort with a huge trumpet. Then I heard her calling me so I had to go.'

'They can't be spies, then,' I said. 'That settles it.'

Harry wasn't convinced. 'Probably there's some-where where Mrs Smith leaves copies of whatever she steals from the Manor. Spies do that. Then another spy picks them up.'

I wondered if she could be right. 'Don't you think we've been a bit stupid – imagining that the secret government people would leave documents all over the place for the cleaner to bring home?'

A cool breeze quivered in the treetops and Max shivered. With one hand, he held on to a sapling as if he might fall over. The thumb of his other hand hovered longingly near his mouth. He was a sad, frightened little boy, even if he was only a year or so younger than us.

'I suppose I ought to tell you,' he said slowly. 'When I first came I overheard Mrs Smith telling her husband about the Manor and she said that there weren't even wastepaper bins to empty. They destroy all the papers or lock them in a safe. The secretaries even take the ribbon things out of their typewriters at night in case anyone could copy from them. And she was saying she had to give references – what are references? – and sign something to say she'd never tell about anything she might see there.'

'Or she'd be shot at dawn, I expect,' Harry said cheerfully. 'Of course, it could have been double-bluff.'

'She didn't know I was listening. I'd heard a noise I thought was a bomb and I was hiding under the table so she didn't know I was there,' he said. 'I'd better go. She has to get up to him in the night.' He began picking his way down the slope to the cottage.

I had a terrible feeling that they were all in danger. I thought of the postman, the builder, the policeman, the Look, Duck and Vanish men – and of Dick Seddon, so angry with the Germans – any Germans, so I ran after Max and clutched his arm. 'Tell them to watch out. There's danger from the village people. There are rumours going round about the Smiths.'

He wasn't listening. 'You're hurting me,' he said, breaking free and running down to the house.

I saw a thread of light showing through the blackout of an upstairs window. Harry had seen it too. 'Come on! We don't want the old man shooting at us!' she called.

'I warned him,' I said as we rode home.

Harry was silent. I think she found it hard to give up

the idea the Smiths were spies and I was a bit sorry, too. It would have been an adventure to capture spies and help win the war. But now we knew more about the Smiths, they'd become real people, not enemies.

'If they're not spies or anything why should they go to one of those camps?' I went on. 'I don't suppose all Germans are horrible like Hitler.'

'Pehaps their son Martin will come back and help them,' Harry said.

'Martin could be dead or he might not come back till the end of the war. We've got to help or Max won't have anyone.'

'How can we stop them? It's like the village has turned the Smiths into Baddies, isn't it?' Harry said. 'After all, they're easier to catch than Hitler.'

Then Bracken shied again as a huge pale owl flew across our path and we both fell off.

By the time we caught Bracken and got home, dirty and slightly bruised, we were too tired to think about anything but sleep.

I tried to creep into the shed but the door creaked and Mum called out, 'Is that you, Pip? Are you all right?'

'Just been to the lav.,' I said – which was true. All the worry had done something funny to my stomach and I only just made it when we got back.

I prayed she wouldn't light the lamp and see I was dressed, but she just said, 'Go to sleep, darling,' and turned over.

I must have slept late because Mum was cooking

breakfast by the time I'd done my best to wipe the dirt off my dungarees and face. 'The Seddons are with Bertha because she's having her piglets,' Mum said. 'Would you like to come to church with me, Pip? You'll have to change, of course. Those dungarees are filthy.'

I was going to say 'no' because I had to talk to Harry about the Smiths but then I saw Mum's face was still blotchy and her eyelids puffed. We never went to church much now I was older because I always complained about the long and boring sermons but maybe Mum felt she needed to pray about Dad. I'd been so wrapped up in Max and the Smiths. It was time I went somewhere with Mum.

'I need a bit of peace.' Her voice was low and sad.

'I'll come,' I said. 'But what about helping here?'

'When we get back. Perhaps Harry would like to come too?'

Then Harry panted in, saying her dad was calling the vet. Big Bertha was having trouble. I explained about church. 'I used to go to the Friends' Meeting – that's the Quakers – sometimes with Mel,' Harry said. 'I don't like all that telling God what to do that goes on in ordinary church. Quakers just sit silently so they can listen to God, Mel says. Sometimes they say things. Ask my mum if she'd like to come with you.'

But Mrs Seddon was flustered and worried about the pig, saying she'd have to wait for the vet. She looked at Mum's little straw hat, blue summer dress and white sandals, brought back from the cottage. 'You'll get dirty going down our lane. I usually harness Silver to the

Governess cart for church and suchlike but there's no time for that today.'

Mum smiled and said she hoped the piglets would be born safely. I admired her for putting on a good act.

I felt funny in a dress instead of trousers. I couldn't be bothered to plait my hair so I just brushed it and wore an Alice band to keep it back. Had I liked or hated being called 'Blondie' the other day? I wasn't sure. It had given me a funny feeling.

As we walked along the dusty track I was silent, but Mum, obviously trying hard for my sake, told me about the wild flowers we saw in the hedgerow, ragged robin, corn cockle, moon-daisies, poppies. 'They remind me of my childhood in the country,' she said. 'So beautiful – they make me want to cry.' But I knew it wasn't because of the flowers.

Golden stubble-fields rolled away into the distance, some patterned with little tents of stacked corn – Harry had told me they were called 'stooks'.

We turned into the village street. Ahead, a single bell tolled mournfully. There weren't any more cheerful peals of church bells now because of the war. A peal of bells meant invasion by the Germans.

'Pip – you're very quiet,' she said. 'Is it because of Daddy?'

Part of it was, of course. The other part of my brain was wondering whether I should tell Mum what the village thought about the Smiths. But what could she do? We were newcomers, after all. I decided it would only worry her.

107

'Are you going to divorce Dad?' I asked abruptly and then wished I hadn't. She stood still and put her fingers to her lips, gathering a smear of her red lipstick on the tip of her white glove.

'It may not come to that. He's . . . fallen in love before and it petered out. I shouldn't be talking to you like this.'

'Before?' I felt a bit sick. 'It's not fair!' I said so loudly that an old couple the other side of the road looked at us.

'Life's not fair,' Mum said. 'He has a weakness, that's all. You mustn't hate him, Pip. Think how brave he is, flying his bomber. And think of all the good times in the past.'

For some reason, I remembered – ages ago – running down Primrose Hill in London with Dad, trying to fly a kite. I always hoped we'd see primroses growing but we never did. He was laughing and as pleased as a small boy when we got it to fly at last.

'I do hate him,' I said, but quietly this time and I don't think she heard because she was waving at Mrs Jarvis as she came out of the Sow and Pigs, dressed for church and wearing a hat like a brown basin.

Seeing the inn sign made me think of poor Bertha. I wondered if having piglets hurt her a lot. I knew all about animals having babies because Josephine Pie had mouselets last year but we didn't need the vet. We moved Joshua to another cage because I'd read in my magazine, *Fur & Feather*, that fathers sometimes killed their young and ate them. Ugh! Maybe they were jealous.

Well, Dad had killed something in me. I didn't love

him any more. I hated his hurting Mum and it was worse that this wasn't the first time he'd fallen in love. That was a stupid expression anyway, I thought, as if you were sliding off a cliff and couldn't stop.

As I sat in church, wedged between Mum and Mrs Jarvis, who said her husband was getting ready for the after-church drinkers, I prayed hard that if my father died it would be quickly and doing something brave so Mum would have a good memory of him.

My mind kept drifting off to think of Dad and of Max so I hardly heard the service – except a bit from the Bible that reminded me of Mr Seddon – something about it was better to have your hand chopped off than do something bad with it. Well, it wasn't fair that he'd had his chopped off when he was trying to do something good. Or was it good to kill people? Perhaps it was all right if they were really evil, like the Nazis, but I thought that probably my father's bombs killed ordinary people and children too as well as Nazis. I just couldn't work it out and gave up.

The Vicar looked like Father Christmas, with a white beard and a pink face. Again my mind drifted off but I caught him saying something about forgiveness – about forgiving someone who'd hurt you ninety-nine times. There was hardly time for Dad to have ninety-nine girl-friends for Mum to forgive.

We prayed for 'our gallant servicemen' and that we might 'defeat the evil forces that seek to rule our wonderful country'. I wondered if the Germans were praying for their gallant servicemen, too. God must be getting sick of so many prayers. And He hadn't done much about the Nazis overrunning Europe and He'd only helped some of the soldiers at Dunkirk to get into boats. I could see why Dick Seddon couldn't believe.

Outside the church, Mum and I were surrounded by Mrs Jarvis, Edie Button, and the Blood brothers, who all asked after my father (as if Mum didn't matter). 'Very brave, those bomber pilots,' said Clem Blood and everyone agreed.

Mum escaped to talk to the Vicar and his wife and the circle round me seemed to close in. 'I hear you brought that boy back to the Smiths,' Mrs Jarvis said, looking at me out of her small blackcurrant eyes. I remembered she didn't like me because of the mice. 'I suppose he's a German too.'

'No . . . ' I began to explain about the Smiths not being spies but they all began talking at once and nobody heard me. 'I told Reg we ought to get those Germans out,' Arthur Blood said. In his Sunday suit and bowler hat he seemed taller and bigger than he had in the shop. 'You heard the Scripture: you have to cut out evil before it grows. Like weeds – or bad bits of meat.' He brought one huge red hand down on another in a chopping motion.

'I don't believe those foreigners really are Martin's parents. I think they're phonies.' Clem Blood's face was an angry purple-red.

'Shouldn't be allowed to stay,' said Edie Button. A breeze was blowing and she brought out a large black pin and savagely skewered her black hat to her hair.

Today she looked more like a witch than a dear old lady.

'My Bertie's going to get some of the LDVs together next week,' Mrs Jarvis whispered.

I thought of the Look, Duck and Vanish men. 'What for?' I managed to say.

She looked at me. '"*Little pitchers have big ears*",' she quoted and the group moved off just as Mum came to tell me it was time to go home.

As we walked back, I wanted to tell her and to ask her what I should do but she was silent and kept dabbing at her eyes with a handkerchief. I just couldn't give her something else to worry about. Harry and I had to help the Smiths ourselves.

Chapter 13

The vet had just come from Felford when we got back, so midday dinner was all upside down, with Mrs Seddon popping out now and again to see how Bertha was doing.

We had chicken stew, fortified with funny-tasting turnips and other vegetables. 'Are we eating poor old Maisie?' Harry asked cheerfully.

It turned out we were. Maisie was one of the oldest of the hens and certainly, she'd had a lot of exercise, judging by her toughness. I was glad I hadn't got to know her, though.

Dick Seddon came in at last. 'Five healthy, two dead,' he pronounced. 'I think Bertha's getting a bit long in the tooth.' Or the snout, I thought, and wondered when we'd be told we were eating 'poor old Bertha'.

I was wondering if we'd have extra time on Sunday, when Harry and I could discuss what to do about the Smiths but we seemed to have more jobs than ever to do, because the morning had been held up over Bertha. Mum and Mrs Seddon washed up and then Mum offered to help Mrs Seddon bottle a heap of ripe plums she'd picked from a tree behind the house. I thought Mum ought to have a rest – she looked exhausted – but I knew she hated giving up, even when she was ill.

I was longing to see the piglets but apparently Bertha and babies had to be quiet for a day or so.

Mrs Seddon had asked us to groom the ponies and check them over. The young colt galloped round the field, bucking and jumping for joy when we came in, but the other ponies were drowsing under the tree, so they were easy to catch.

'Max could ride Tiny, couldn't he?' I said, as I brushed the small pony's mane and tail. 'He's so small and thin.'

Harry sighed. 'Dad would never let him,' she said.

'We've got to find out if they really are going to attack the Smiths.' I told Harry what I had overheard after church.

'It might be just talk. Besides, it would have to be official, wouldn't it? The police would have to arrest them.'

'Mrs Jarvis said next week. I think we ought to warn the Smiths. Perhaps they could hide or something,' I suggested.

Harry tied Bracken more tightly to the post in case he nipped, and picked up his foreleg. 'This shoe's a bit worn. About the Smiths, I don't think they'll believe us – because we're young. Besides, where will they go?'

'They could hide up in the den.' I knew it was impractical as I said it.

'For how long? They can't just leave all their things. And what about the dotty old man? He'd probably want to shoot it out, like in a cowboy film.' She put down Bracken's foreleg and went to sit on an upturned bucket. 'It might be mostly talk. We've got to find out for sure what's going to happen.'

'They're hardly likely to tell us, are they? Couldn't we tell PC Thorogood that we're certain the Smiths aren't spies?'

Harry ran her fingers through her hair so it stood up all over her head. 'Come off it, Pip! Use your bloody brain for once. All we know is what Max told us and he isn't truthful, is he? He lied about his mother being dead and he sort of lied about Mrs Smith being horrible to him. We don't even know if he's warned them, like you told him to. And they probably wouldn't believe him.'

I felt cross with Harry. I wasn't stupid! After all, I'd passed the Scholarship exam for the Grammar School, hadn't I? Also I was cross with myself because I hadn't said anything to defend the Smiths after church this morning, not that it would have helped much because I was just another evacuee to the people of Hogsty End, not one of them.

I went to see how Mum was getting on, with the vague idea I might somehow think of a way of telling her and Mrs Seddon.

The kitchen was full of steam and the smell of fruit. Mum, still wearing her apron, was asleep in the old rocking chair by the range. A row of bottled plums stood on the table. I could hear the Seddons talking in the bedroom above us. Dick Seddon's voice suddenly rose. I couldn't hear the words but he sounded angry.

I looked at Mum, once so full of energy and hope. Now she looked small and defeated. Again I realised it wouldn't be fair to worry her about the Smiths.

I went to see the mice. Somehow they calmed me down because they'd been with me when we moved. In the distance, I saw Harry with young Goldie trotting round her on a long rein. She didn't see me and I was glad, for once. I needed to be on my own.

Two farm cats were crouched on our step. I suppose they smelled mice inside the hut. They ran off when I shouted at them and then I was sorry. Mice and rats were their dinner, after all. It would be like shouting at me when I ate meat.

I fed the mice with oatmeal and little bits of chopped up apple and carrot taken from the ponies' bucket. Joshua came out of hiding and sat, delicately nibbling a piece of apple, held between his tiny pink paws. Josephine scattered her food untidily and then came to run up my arm and sit on my shoulder, tickling my ear with her quivering whiskers.

'I don't know what to do,' I told the mice. I felt powerless to help the Smiths. If only I was older... thirteen was a silly, in-between age when the adults thought you were still a child, not to be taken seriously.

I wished I could just stay there, hiding away from any decisions, safe with the mice.

I removed Josephine from her perch and put her back, checking their water-pot. I wandered restlessly round the hut, thinking I'd find a book until it was time for high tea and all the evening chores.

I pulled out books from Mel's shelf: as well as *Little Women* she had several of the same books as I had, like *The Wind in the Willows*, which made me feel closer to her, in a way. A fat black exercise book fell out and lay open on the wooden floor. It was filled with neat, rounded writing in black ink. The date was last September – 1939 – when the war began.

115

The Friends don't believe in fighting – just passive resistance. They say Jesus told us not to kill. Dad doesn't understand what I feel and he is leaving to fight. I don't know if I'm right. What would I do if Germans or anyone came to the farm and tried to kill Mum or Harry? Wouldn't I want to run at them with a pitchfork? Could I stop myself? I am going to train to be a nurse but isn't nursing in a way helping the war and hiding from definite action? Pacifists in the last war were put in prison because of their beliefs but Quakers went to the battlefields and helped the wounded ...

I would have gone on reading only Mum put her head round the door and said tea was ready. I guiltily put the book back. It must be Mel's diary before she went away and I knew I'd hate anyone reading mine.

I wondered what I'd do if someone attacked Mum – or even Thomasina and the mice. If I was brave enough, I knew I'd go for them, whatever I believed. And wasn't that natural? Even animals didn't like strangers invading their homes: like the farm cat chasing poor Thomasina away. After all, *I* knew Thomasina was a gentle, fat cat but the farm cats might have thought she was a nasty invader. Harry had told me that she thought there were new kittens in the hay-barn. The farm cats' instincts were to defend them at all costs. But of course they'd never heard of Quakers or passive resistance, had they?

Suddenly life seemed so complicated; nothing was black and white, only grey.

Chapter 14

Nurse Robin was already in the farmhouse, changing Dick Seddon's dressings and she was to stay for tea.

Mrs Seddon warned her that we were only having scrambled goose eggs and a little ham but Nurse Robin seemed delighted. 'It's a nice change from the Sow and Pigs – I mean, Mrs Jarvis does her best but she has to help at the bar so things get burned. I'll be glad to get back to my cottage but it's going to take a while to repair. By the way,' she leaned forward. 'I've heard there's a kind of meeting there tonight – about those Germans at Keeper's Cottage.'

Dick Seddon looked up from his food. 'I'll be there. Time we got rid of them. Probably spies.'

Mum looked surprised. 'I didn't know they were Germans or is it just a rumour?'

She'd not heard the after-church discussion. I kicked Harry under the table. It was time to speak. 'I heard they're nationalised British,' I said.

'Do you mean "naturalised", Pip?' Mum asked, smiling. 'How do you know?'

'Once a German always a German,' Dick Seddon muttered. 'Want to rule the world, they do, and they don't mind how they do it. If you'd watched them fly low over the Dunkirk beaches, machine-gunning everyone, even the wounded, you'd know what scum they are.'

Mrs Seddon plonked a bowl of stewed plums on the table. 'Look – I've got gypsy blood and people say gypsies are a thieving lot. Well, I'm not a thief. So I reckon not all Germans can be bad.' She tossed her black plait over her shoulder defiantly as she went to fetch the custard.

'Pacifist talk. You ought to watch your tongue, woman!' Dick Seddon said, and he strode out of the room, pushing his chair back so hard that it fell over.

We heard the front door slam. Nurse Robin looked anxious. 'Did I say the wrong thing? He's not really fit enough to go walking. I'll keep an eye on him.' She went off in a hurry.

I imagined that Dick Seddon would be very impatient with anyone who tried to stop him doing what he wanted.

As soon as we'd helped with the dishes, I whispered to Harry, 'We've got to get to that meeting at the pub.'

The bats had begun their nightly flight in the dusk by the time we'd shut up Auntie and the hens.

'We'll get into trouble,' Harry said but we were already on the way, running down the rutty lane to the village.

The first stars were showing when we reached the pub. 'They won't let us in,' Harry said.

'I'll pretend we forgot something – a pen or something, when we stayed there. Then once we're in, we can hide under a table or something.' I was quite proud of the idea.

Men were going into the pub by the main door but we knocked on the side door. After a longish time, Mrs

118

Jarvis came, looking hot and flustered. 'What do you want?' she asked crossly. 'We're very busy tonight.'

'Mum wonders if she left her fountain pen here,' I blurted out. It was a lie but in a good cause.

'I'd have seen it – these rooms get thoroughly cleaned, you know,' Mrs Jarvis said, half shutting the door.

'It might have rolled under the bed,' I said quickly. 'Into a crack in the boards.'

'Oh all right. Come and look but quickly. I've got to get back to the bar. Does it need two of you to search for a pen? Shall I tell your dad you're here?' she asked Harry.

Luckily she didn't wait for an answer and we followed her into the public bar towards the staircase at the back of the inn. Dick Seddon had his back to us as he talked to a group of men, including the Blood brothers, Reg Thorogood and Percy the postman. 'They need to be rooted out,' he was saying as we slipped past and through the big oak door. Harry left it open, just a crack. There were coats hanging in the back hall and she pulled me under a big overcoat.

We listened. There was a lot of talk about Germans and spies and the boy who'd run off from the Smiths. Dick Seddon kept on saying loudly, 'They're stinking Germans. We don't want them here.'

I heard Reg Thorogood's loud, slow voice saying, 'I need to get authority first,' then the other men all talked at once, almost shouting him down.

'By tomorrow then,' I heard Dick Seddon say. 'Sooner the better.'

'What on earth are you children doing, hiding there?' Mrs Jarvis was upon us, angrily pulling aside the coats and macs.

'Just a game,' Harry said in a meek voice.

'Surely you're too old for hide-and-seek? Did you find the pen? I didn't hear you go upstairs.'

Somehow we got out, muttering excuses, but this time Dick Seddon turned and saw us. 'What are you doing here, Harry?' He sounded really angry.

'Something Pippa's mum forgot...' she muttered and we fled.

'Now we'll be in trouble,' I said. 'Mum hates lies.'

Then I thought hadn't she sort of lied to me, about everything being all right with her and Dad and all the time knowing about his girlfriends?

'I think the best thing is to go to bed early and pretend to be asleep,' Harry said as we jogged back, through the dusk. 'In case my dad tells your mum that you were at the pub.'

Suddenly a motorbike swooped past us, then stopped.

A man got off and strode towards us. 'Better run,' Harry said. 'Mum said we mustn't talk to strangers.'

But Don's deep voice stopped us. 'Want a lift?' he said and in no time at all we were both squashed behind him, clinging on and bumping up the lane.

'Can't you go faster?' Harry asked. 'When I'm older, I shall buy a motorbike.'

I'd have liked it better if there had been more room on the bike – my head was jammed against Don's leather jacket and Harry's spiky hair tickled my neck. And it was very bumpy!

Just before the farm, we met Mum, walking down the lane towards us. Her pale blue dress glimmered in the fading light.

Don braked, so quickly that Harry flattened me against him.

'Hiya, Alice!' Don said. 'I found these two girls straying away from home! Maybe they've been meeting some young guys...' He was laughing but Harry made an angry noise.

'I was getting worried about you both,' Mum said but I saw her teeth gleaming in the dusk and she was actually smiling – because of Don, of course.

'I'm off duty tonight,' he said. 'I came to take you for a spin on Rosemarie. She's mine, you know, I bought her when I came over.'

'Well, I'm not quite sure...' Mum began.

'Lucky you,' Harry said. 'I'll go if you don't want to.'

'Mum needs cheering up,' I said.

'We'll only be gone an hour – to the next village. I don't know its name because it's been blacked out! There's a real beauty of an old pub there – wonderful old beams, nothing like it at home.'

At last she said she'd go, just for an hour, if I promised to stay at the farm.

As soon as they'd roared off in a cloud of exhaust, Harry said, 'He's OK.'

'Yes. Couldn't we ask him what to do about the Smiths?'

'No. He'd not want to get involved,' Harry said.

121

'Remember, he's a foreigner, too, and he'd not want to clash with the villagers.'

I wrote in my diary that night: *We heard them plotting at the pub to get the Smiths out. Harry and me had a long discussion (actually it was more of an argument) and we're going to warn the Smiths tomorrow as soon as we can get away. Mum's still out with Don. I hope he cheers her up so she can forget my horrible father.*

Then I was too sleepy to write any more. I must have slept deeply because I didn't hear Mum coming to bed.

We were having breakfast the next day when the geese honked an alarm outside and there was a bang on the door.

Dick Seddon's face was twisted with pain as he took his pills, Mum was cutting up bread and Mrs Seddon was busy frying eggs and bacon. Harry and I went to the door.

A telegraph boy stood there, smart in his blue uniform with the jaunty cap and the red stripe down the trousers. 'Telegram for Mrs Armstrong,' he said.

My stomach churned as I took the brown envelope. Telegrams always meant something was wrong.

Mum's hands shook as she opened it.

'It's from the War Office,' she whispered. 'They say Daddy's "missing, presumed dead".'

She sat down suddenly as if her legs wouldn't hold her up.

Time seemed to stop in the kitchen as if the people were playing musical statues. Mrs Seddon held her frying pan, Dick Seddon's hand stopped on the way to his mouth and Harry just stared at Mum.

I felt hot and cold and the room seemed to tilt sideways. As I fell into darkness I knew I'd killed Dad.

Chapter 15

I woke up on a scratchy sofa in the never-used front room. Mum was bending over me and the others crowded round but I took no notice of them. 'He got killed because I wanted him to die,' I whispered to Mum.

The others melted away tactfully.

She gave me a hug. 'Don't be so silly, darling. His plane was shot down. People don't die because you want them to. Besides, it was only because you were angry with him. I know you didn't mean it.'

I knew I did but now I'd succeeded I just felt guilty. Also sad because he was my father, after all.

'It just says "Missing, presumed dead",' Mum said. 'He'd have a parachute. He could have escaped.'

But I saw the plane belching out fire and smoke as it plunged down. I just knew he was dead and it was my fault.

When we went back to the kitchen, Dick Seddon unexpectedly gave Mum an awkward hug, keeping his painful stump out of the way. 'Bloody Huns!' he muttered.

Only Harry had an appetite for the eggs and bacon. Mrs Seddon made me drink a cup of sweet tea and told Mum to have a lie-down.

Mum dabbed at her eyes. 'No – I shall go and work in the canteen as usual. It will do me good and after all, there's a war on!' she finished with a sad little smile.

I'd liked to have talked to her but she made up her face, tied her hair in a scarf and walked off, her head held high.

As I helped Harry and Mrs Seddon with the usual farm chores, I thought about Dad. Had he died quickly? Had he thought about us as the plane hurtled down? Had he been sorry about loving Netta and hurting Mum? Or was he just so terrified he didn't think at all?

I couldn't really believe he was dead. Perhaps it was because he was so tall and energetic, he seemed to be larger than life. People looked at him when he came into a room – especially women, of course.

Then I thought of his bad side. The time when we flew the kite was a special one, but usually he was either away or had some excuse for not coming to see me in the school Nativity play, or joining in trips to the Zoo at weekends or long walks and picnics on Hampstead Heath. So he'd only been half a dad – or perhaps just a quarter. And when he was there he went on at us about things and never seemed to listen.

I plodded round, dimly aware that Mrs Seddon had gone in to get lunch.

'I've found out where that goose is laying,' Harry called. 'Come over here, Pip.'

The goose eggs were hidden in the bushes at the side of the field, four of them, twice as big as hens' eggs. As we watched, there was a cracking sound and a small beak came through the white shell. I crouched, transfixed with excitement as a bedraggled gosling chipped its way out and stood, cheeping and damp.

Then the mother goose was running towards us, her

wings and neck outstretched and we retreated quickly.

'I've never seen that before,' I said. 'Wasn't it exciting?'

'At least you don't look so sad,' Harry said. 'After all, Pip, you said you hated your dad for going off with that girl. Now your mum will be free to see men like Don. You might get a much better father in the long run. Anyway, we've got to get away somehow to warn the Smiths. Why don't you say you'd like to have a ride to take your mind off things? Then we could go off this afternoon.'

'I still don't see what the Smiths can do to escape,' I said. 'What we ought to do is stop your dad going there. I bet he's the leader.'

Harry pulled at her hair – I'd noticed she did this when she was worried. 'It sounded as if they wanted the police to be involved and Reg Thorogood said he needed permission or something. So PC Thorogood's the leader, in a way.'

I felt a bit desperate. 'Let's just tell your dad at lunch-time about Mr Smith fighting in the First World War.'

'He'd say it was lies and they'd all wonder how you knew when they think all you did was to take Max home. They'll be angry if they knew we hid Max in the den,' Harry said.

Dick Seddon was very kind to me when we came in for the meal. He kept saying things like: 'Got to keep your chin up for your mother's sake, Pippa,' and 'You never know, your father could be alive after all.' Somehow it was impossible to go on at him about the Smiths.

He left early, anyway, while I was still thinking what

126

to say. He said he'd been invited to an LDV parade at the village hall. 'They think I can pass on some of my military knowledge.' He sounded pleased and said he could manage the walk very well, with his stick.

Harry and I looked at each other. Was this just an ordinary meeting or was Dick Seddon going to spread the rumours against the Smiths?

Mrs Seddon said she had some shopping to do and she'd take him to the Hall, all the same. She asked Harry to harness up Silver. 'We've got to save petrol,' she explained to me. I thought she was probably going to see her husband didn't overdo it.

Harry muttered that she was going to take me out on Bracken, to cheer me up, and Mrs Seddon looked pleased. 'You can take turns riding,' she suggested.

By the time we'd washed up and harnessed Silver, it was mid-afternoon on a perfect early September day. Already long shadows fell across the fields and there was a smell of wood smoke; someone's bonfire would have to be put out before nightfall.

I sat on the pony behind Harry. 'Have you thought what we're going to say?' I asked as we rode through the woods.

'Anything to make them listen. Maybe they've got documents or something to prove they aren't still Germans,' Harry said.

Bracken, burdened again with both of us, was in a lazy mood and snatched at leaves and grass. Harry had to keep on urging him along so it seemed a long way back to Keeper's Cottage.

Again we tied the pony to a branch and went down the path. Again the curtains were drawn and the house looked dead. 'Perhaps they've gone away,' I said hopefully. I had this awful feeling that Dad's death wasn't the last of the dreadful things that would happen.

As we knocked, Harry stepped back from the porch and said, 'The gun!'

I joined her and saw the glint of metal from the upstairs window. 'If he's ill he won't be strong enough to shoot,' I was saying when Max opened the door.

'Go away!' he shouted. 'Mr Smith's shut himself in his room because the policeman called this morning and upset him. Now we can't get him to unlock the door.'

Mrs Smith joined him. She looked white and scared. 'Please go,' she said.

'We've come to warn you that the Local Defence Volunteers and others may be coming along soon to get you out because you're Germans,' I said quickly.

'We've got a place where you can hide in the woods,' Harry began.

'I can't leave him,' Mrs Smith said. 'Besides, we have a right to be here. I tried to explain to that PC Thorogood but he is not so clever, is he? I don't think he understood. If only our Martin would come home.'

Winston began to howl from his kennel followed by the awful wail of the air-raid warning, echoed by others, further away, like a cats' orchestra. Then we heard the uneven throb of planes.

We ran a few paces back and looked up.

The sky seemed black with planes flying above the

clearing, like great dark birds of death, so low that I could see the black crosses. I felt glued to the ground with fear and Harry was statue-still.

Suddenly Mr Smith pushed past his wife and was outside, wearing a nightshirt and carrying his gun. He shouted something in German and fired straight up at the nearest plane.

We heard Mrs Smith calling, 'Hans, Hans!' and she ran out, dragging him back to the cottage.

'Come with us!' Harry shouted but only Max followed us – the Smiths disappeared into the cottage. Max screamed as he clung to my hand, racing to the shelter of the bushes.

'Lie down!' Harry ordered but I looked back and heard a noise like a sheet being ripped in two as a bomb fell from one of the planes and hit the cottage.

I know I screamed but I thought I heard an echo from the cottage. Then I saw a bright white light flashing out of the hole in the roof followed by clouds of white smoke.

'We've got to save them!' I yelled and began to run back down the path. The planes still rumbled overhead but I didn't think about them. I just thought of the Smiths in a burning house.

I opened the front door and more smoke belched out. I reeled back, coughing, bumping into Harry and Max just behind me.

Max was screaming, 'Mum, Mum!' as he dodged past us and went straight into the house. He must be half-crazy with shock, dazed into believing this was the other raid when his mother died.

129

Harry ran after him and I followed. I could only see white smoke which filled my lungs and stung my eyes. Two dark figures came towards us.

'Go outside,' Mrs Smith coughed, pulling Max along. 'Hans has shut himself in his room and won't come out.' She gasped as we all retreated into the garden, spluttering and coughing.

There was a silence and I looked up. The planes were just a distant rumble and at that moment the long note of the All Clear sounded.

Then I saw the old man outlined against the bright light of the fire as he opened the upstairs window. He tried to call out but all you could hear was a gurgling cry as he fell back.

'Ladder?' Harry asked.

'The back,' said Mrs Smith.

The ladder was an ancient wooden one but quite long. We dragged it round to the front of the cottage and propped it against the wall. It was a few feet short of the attic window. 'I'll go,' Harry said but I had my foot on the bottom rung. I hated heights but somehow in my mind, curdled with fear, I knew I had to punish myself for Dad's death and rescue Hans Smith. Afterwards I realised I'd been dotty to think I could do it but at the time it seemed the only thing to do.

'I'm coming too,' Harry said but the ladder was shaking already under my weight.

'Don't! Just hold it,' I yelled, my throat sore with the smoke.

I looked up and the flames were licking along the

roof, from the bomb-hole in the middle, flames greedily growing all the time.

I was nearly at the top and I dared not look down. But how could I get from the top of the ladder and over the sill? I called, 'Mr Smith!' but he didn't answer. He must have collapsed on the attic floor and I knew I couldn't possibly get in and carry him to safety – I wasn't strong enough. Tears poured down my face and I found myself crying out, 'Dad – I didn't want you to die!'

Suddenly there were great shouts from below. 'Come down, girl!' called a man's voice, so commanding that I obeyed.

Going down was worse than climbing up and I'm ashamed to say that I shut my eyes at one point as I moved hands and feet automatically.

Arms pulled me off the lowest rung and a man was climbing the ladder now. Dick Seddon was shouting, 'Fetch water from the well!' and there they were, the Volunteers in their uniforms: I recognised the Blood brothers, Mr Jarvis, Percy the postman and PC Thorogood. I saw the sticks and guns they'd dropped on the ground and I knew why they'd really come.

There were only two buckets. Harry pumped the water and Dick Seddon organised the LDVs to chuck it inside the hall.

I couldn't see which LDV was at the top of the ladder now but he shouted down something about 'too hot,' as he tried to reach up and hold the sill. I was holding Max, who was struggling to get away when I saw Dick Seddon disappear into the house.

'Dad!' Harry shouted. 'Stop him! He's too crippled to help!' Someone held her back as she tried to run after her father, just as the Blood brothers followed him inside the cottage.

Then it was all confusion: fire; smoke; Mrs Smith clutching at Max beside me and people shouting as the roof flamed above the trees, a sure signal for more German planes. I was past being frightened; it felt unreal, like a film. 'Winston,' Max said and ran off. I followed him to the kennel next to the burning cottage. We undid the terrified dog and I did my best to hang on to him as we ran back to see a fire engine, bell clanging, coming up the path from the village.

Chapter 16

Then the men came out of the cottage door coughing. Two of them were carrying a limp body, which they lowered to the ground. The light of the fire showed Dick Seddon, collapsing next to the body.

Max fell into my arms, crying for his mother. I let Winston go and took Max away down the path, where he couldn't see the burning cottage. I made him sit down and he hid his face against my shoulder, his thin body shaking although the early evening was warm.

Winston must have followed us because he came to sit by Max, sniffing and licking at his face. I found myself talking about anything but the fire, about the farm, the new piglets, watching the gosling hatch. Gradually, Max's sobs slowed down and I found his head on my lap. He was fast asleep.

I just sat, my back against a tree-trunk, the dog's furry warmth against us and my thoughts all muddled up. I kept seeing what had happened in flashbacks – the planes above – Mr Smith in his white nightshirt – my awful fear on the ladder – Dick Seddon running into the house . . . and those guns and sticks thrown down on the grass.

'Pippa!' In a kind of dream I looked up and saw the Seddons' truck, Mrs Seddon and Mum inside.

The truck stopped and they both jumped out. 'Are you

all right?' asked Mum, rushing to me as I staggered to my feet, my legs numb from Max's weight.

'Where's Dick?' asked Mrs Seddon.

As soon as I told her, she ran to the fire, whose glow we could see through the trees.

'We heard the alarm and saw the planes coming over from the canteen,' Mum said. 'The men went back on duty at once – the message given out at the canteen was that the German planes were on their way to London but they were dropping incendiary bombs on the way. I was so scared for you and the farm. Don wasn't there so I hitched a lift back and found Mrs Seddon had a message from Mrs Jarvis that the men had gone to Keeper's Cottage and you and Harry were in the woods. So she got out the truck. And then we could see the smoke ... ' She gave a little gasp. Max, addled with shock, clung to her.

'The bloomin' Germans got my great-uncle Hans,' he said, tears dripping down his face.

I couldn't settle that night although I was so tired. Nurse Robin had been to see Dick Seddon, who'd refused to go to hospital. He hadn't got burned but coughed all the time from the smoke in his lungs and eventually a doctor turned up from Felford to check him over. Bracken had trotted back on his own.

I looked at Max, asleep on an old mattress with Winston taking up the biggest part. Max's thumb was in his mouth and he was clutching my old teddy, Rupert. His gran's black handbag was beside the mattress and he'd propped up a photograph of his parents, arm in arm, smiling.

I wrote: *They are calling it the Blitz and it started today with a big attack on London. The German planes dropped some bombs on the way just to scare people I suppose and an incendiary bomb hit the Smiths' cottage and started a fire. The LDVs and firemen saved some of the cottage but Hans Smith is dead. I couldn't believe it but some of the men who'd come to get the Smiths put in prison offered Mrs Smith and Max a bed in their homes. Was it because they felt guilty? Mum asked if Max could come to the farm as I'd told her we knew him and Harry told her father that Mrs Smith must come too. Harry had seen the guns and sticks lying around near the cottage and she asked her father what they were for (she knew of course). That's called blackmail – I think. Anyway he said yes. So Mrs Smith's on the prickly sofa in the front room with Mrs Seddon's best pink eiderdown over her. The doctor gave her something to help her sleep. I bet Dick Seddon changes his mind about having Mrs Smith and Max. He's burned up with hate like a fire. Would it go out so quickly?*

PC Thorogood came round and talked to Mrs Smith (who is called Ulla). Harry asked him why all the men had come and he said it was to rescue the Smiths. Then she said why did they bring guns and sticks? PC Thorogood went a bit pale and sweaty-looking and said the LDVs were on an exercise. Then he said Mrs Smith won't need to go to a prison because she applied ages ago to be British so she was telling the truth. Mrs Smith

*said her husband had medals from the First World War
when he fought for England.*

*Now I feel very tired but I sort of ache everywhere and
I still feel guilty about Dad. There was actually a
telephone call for Mum at the farm from Don but I don't
know what he said. She's talking to Mrs Seddon and I
think they want to be left alone.*

*I've got even worse feelings about the black pit under
our feet. When the everyday ice cracks we fall in.*

Chapter 17

'So you needn't feel guilty,' Harry said as we waited for the bus. We were going to Felford Grammar School and I was almost as scared as I'd been up the ladder. Lucky Max, allowed to go to the cosy little village school even though he was eleven because Mrs Seddon just said firmly he wasn't fit enough for the eight-mile journey.

I didn't like the uniform: a sack-like gym-slip in black over a white shirt and a dreary black blazer which was much too hot in the September sunshine. And there were the horrible felt hats which we had to wear every day to school. And stockings! I'd never worn them before – they were black and thick and held up with an awful elastic thing called a suspender belt.

We carried our gas masks and Mum had made sure there was a proper shelter at the school. I hoped the lessons would be interrupted a lot.

'I do sort of feel guilty still,' I said. 'And anyway – now Mum can't do anything with Dad in prisoner-of-war camp. He's sort of neither dead nor alive.'

'At least he won't have Netta there. He might forget her and want your mum when he gets out.'

'I don't think I want him back. And I'm not sure Mum does, either. Don's coming to see Mum next leave he gets but he's been posted further away. And flying

137

Spitfires is very dangerous. Don could get shot down.'
Nothing in life was certain except perhaps the animals
on the farm and they got eaten.

Mrs Smith had just heard that Martin had been
captured after Dunkirk. 'Perhaps your dad and Martin
Smith will meet in prison camp,' Harry said.

'I think there are masses of prison camps,' I said.
'Your dad thinks the war won't be finished by Christmas
after all because of the Blitz. Mum said she saw the red
glow of London burning from the top of Boar's Hill.' I
wondered if our flat in London was bombed or burned
and I imagined dying in a fire. It was too near what had
happened recently so I switched my mind off and went
on talking. 'Maybe I'll be almost grown up by the time
Dad comes back. Or maybe we might lose the war, then
what would happen?'

'I'll miss Max when the Smiths go back to the
cottage,' Harry said. 'He loves the animals. Just as well
as he's not heard anything about his father.'

'They must think a lot of Mrs Smith at the Manor to
get all those workmen to rebuild the place,' I said,
hitching at my stockings. 'Maybe she wasn't just a
cleaner...'

'Maybe. At least my dad talks to her sometimes.'
Harry kicked at the dirt with her scruffy lace-up shoes.
'But he still hates all Germans.'

I saw two boys running towards us, one hobbling a
bit: satchels and gas masks thumping on their backs. 'I
thought Spike might be needed on the farm.'

'I still hate Spike,' Harry said. 'But Benny's OK.'

Spike ran up. He stared at us. 'Right poshed-up, aren't you? Fancy us having to travel to school with you, Skinny Blondie and Hairless Harry!' He grabbed both our hats and threw them into the road under the wheels of the approaching bus.

Harry hit him with her gas mask. He reeled, clutching his nose. 'Not again!' he shouted.

'Don't miss the bus!' Harry yelled back. I thought I heard Benny laugh as we all got on.

We might win the war one day but I knew there would always be people who would start wars or put you in prison camps if you were foreign or different, because they thought their country should rule the world. Could Mel and her Quakers alter anything?

I wondered if Harry would stick up for me if the bullies at the new school ganged up against me. I wasn't at all sure. But I knew what had happened since we came to the farm had changed me. I'd thought the war was just a nuisance before but now I knew there were masses of children who'd lost their parents and homes, who'd really fallen into the dark pit. So going to a new school was nothing, really.

'Hurry up, you bloody kids!' the ticket collector shouted. 'Don't you know there's a war on?'